BEST
DEBUT
SHORT
STORIES
2025

Judges

Lydi Conklin

Dionne Irving

Brenda Peynado

CATAPULT
NEW YORK

BEST DEBUT SHORT STORIES

2025

The PEN America Dau Prize

Edited by Kendall Storey
and Elizabeth Pankova

BEST DEBUT SHORT STORIES 2025

First Catapult edition: 2025

Please see permissions on page 235 for individual credits.

ISBN: 978-1-64622-315-2

Library of Congress Control Number: 2021936334

Cover design by Nicole Caputo
Cover illustration © Sirin Thada

Catapult
New York, NY
books.catapult.co

Printed in the United States of America

10 9 8 7 6 5 4 3 2 1

CONTENTS

Introduction
Kendall Storey and Elizabeth Pankova, series editors —— *ix*

Burrowing Creatures | Steven Archer
AGNI ——————————————————————— 3

Invert | Samantha Barrett
Foglifter ——————————————————— 23

Faultline | brandon brown
Split Lip Magazine ————————————— 47

Corn Soup | Sammi Chiyao
Peatsmoke Journal ————————————— 51

Elastic | Joanna Demkiewicz
Midwest Review ———————————————— 71

Lovesick | Jason Fernandes
North American Review ——————————— 91

The Faraday Cage | Lara Hughes
The Arkansas International———————————115

A Resting Place | Celine Ipek
McSweeney's Quarterly ———————————————— 143

Mouth and Heart | Jessie Li
StoryQuarterly ———————————————————— 154

The Diaspora Café | Vince Omni
Michigan Quarterly Review ————————————— 174

Little Women | Megan Tennant
The Common ————————————————————— 199

Ride Me Up to Heaven | Zhenglong Yang
StoryQuarterly ———————————————————— 212

About the Judges ————————————————— 229
About the PEN/Robert J. Dau Prize ——————— 231
List of Participating Publications ———————— 233
Permissions ——————————————————————— 235

INTRODUCTION

A WRITER OF SHORT FICTION, LIKE ANY MINIATURIST, must be skilled in the art of illusion. The best short stories feel like peeking into the keyhole of a well-furnished, long lived-in home, only to step away and realize it's a dollhouse. They are compact and restricted, but the space they uncover and fill in our minds knows no bounds.

It's not surprising that writers have long bemoaned the challenges of the short story, of crafting an enticing, robust, meaningful world in so few words. It's a delicate balance of proportion that requires the constant question of "How much?" How much time to spend on a scene? How much context to give to a conflict? How much backstory to a character? How much certainty to an ending? Not too much! But also, please, just enough to keep us readers interested, to make the act of filling in the emotional and narrative blanks a pleasurable one.

And so, it is a joy to introduce this year's anthology of *Best Debut Short Stories: The PEN America Dau Prize*, a set of wonderfully unique dollhouses, each offering a peek into a vivid miniature realm. Their authors have chosen various methods of construction: some sweep through decades, some focus on a singular moment; some conceal the name of their protagonist, some give voice to two narrators; some see a character through a life-altering event, others introduce them only after they've begun reeling from its consequences. All of them, however, succeed in surprising and engaging us in profound questions of identity, bodily autonomy, margin-alization, grief, and community. They cleverly pair begrudging opposites—an unsuccessful father with his ambitious child, a tentative queer woman with an eager new partner, a competitive dancer with her newly dysfunctional body. They plunge us into unfamiliar environments—off-grid communities, eerie meditation getaways for the wealthy, near futures where people take pills to stay in their relationships.

Many of the stories in this anthology exchange the tired subject of love for the slippery chimera of intimacy. They examine the kind of closeness that can coexist with resentment, fear, boredom—even hate—but binds people together, nonetheless. Whether between parents and children, spouses, adulterers, siblings, or even past and present selves, the shape-shifting uncertainty of intimacy drives narrative tension and forges openings for reader interpretation.

Sammi Chiyao's "Corn Soup" and Jessie Li's "Mouth and Heart" both explore the uneasy dynamic between a child and a parent who has gravely disappointed them. In the former, a daughter must overcome her anger to help her mother acclimate after she is released from prison for defrauding people. In the latter, a high-achieving daughter looks back and reckons with her lifelong disdain for her meek, professionally failed father. In each story, the return path to normal parental love feels untraversable. The protagonist of "Mouth and Heart" arrives at her estranged father's hospital bedside when he is already nonresponsive. While her mother was in prison, the narrator of "Corn Soup" experienced the irreversible pain of her father's death. And yet there are tiny glimpses of redemption. Cooking the titular corn soup, once a prison comfort, becomes the crack in the silence between mother and daughter. In Li's story, the daughter's memory of her father's oft-repeated proverb becomes a beacon for connection in a realm beyond language: "Knife of a mouth, tofu of a heart."

Sometimes, familial relationships are defined by the departure of one of its members, and the new ways of organizing life that must be constructed in their wake. After her husband's sudden death, the mother at the center of "The Faraday Cage" unknowingly moves with her son to an off-grid community of radiation-fearing West Virginians. The shield her son begins to construct for their paranoid neighbor mirrors the safety and security both he and his mother so achingly desire in their new family configuration. In "Burrowing Creatures," the son of a financially struggling immigrant father and recently deceased mother seeks comfort and communion in the burrows of turtles and hermit crabs, despite the overwhelming cruelty of the world they inhabit.

In romantic relationships, intimacy is not just a current state but an accumulation that hurtles couples toward the future. But can this careening progress be called "love"? Jason Fernandes's "Lovesick," in which couples enshrine the honeymoon phase by beginning to take a love drug a year into their relationship, is a delightfully anxious confrontation with this question. In its strange but familiar world, people desperately want to hurtle into the future unscathed, with their seatbelts on. Unfortunately, there are no such panaceas in Zhenglong Yang's "Ride Me Up to Heaven," where a pregnancy, the ultimate symbol of potential, seems doomed from the start, borne of a wife's desperate affair with a sex shop owner to escape her gay husband's indifference. Their shared pain and fear for the life soon to come is the closest thing to a love drug they will get, and it will have to suffice. The young woman in Megan

Tennant's "Little Women" asks herself similar questions about what brings and keeps people together. Her religious family and her soon-to-be-married sister seem to have the answers, but her own romantic experience leaves her uncertain. In Celine Ipek's "A Resting Place," the protagonist's marriage has opened a future of frivolous luxury, and yet somehow, her former self who lived in a windowless apartment is not able to fully meet the demands of her new reality. When a local community fixture in Vince Omni's "The Diaspora Café" seems destined to be swallowed by a corporate chain, its owner must decide whether to stay true to her principles and her family.

In fact, in a world where the self is increasingly fractured—whether through migration, or media presence, or psychological trauma—this intimacy, between the different iterations of our own bodies and minds, is perhaps the most significant and ripe for exploration. "Invert" by Samantha Barrett, "Faultline" by brandon brown, and "Elastic" by Joanna Demkiewicz all consider the mysterious and overwhelming power of embodiment. Barrett's story follows a trans woman reckoning with the ghost of her former self and the terrifying potential of her future one. "Faultline," in striking, poetic prose, gives a glimpse into the intense transformative potential of a first physical encounter. In "Elastic," a young dancer who experiences a sudden and debilitating illness must redefine her relationship with her body, which has thus far dictated the rest of her identity.

The resonances between the twelve stories in this collection are at once a magical coincidence and a testament to the attention and care with which the authors have observed and responded to the difficult, sometimes depraved, sometimes hopeful moment we live in. It is an exciting honor to get to publish them together.

Thank you to this year's judges, Lydi Conklin, Dionne Irving, and Brenda Peynado, who selected these stories from a long list of admirable submissions and put together both a wonderfully cohesive and individually strong anthology. Thank you as ever to PEN America and the Robert Jensen Dau Foundation. Finally, thank you to the journals in this year's anthology, and the editors who were the first to notice and give voice to the talent within this book's pages.

Kendall Storey
Elizabeth Pankova
Series Editors

BEST
DEBUT
SHORT
STORIES

2025

Editor's Note

There's a kind of shape-shifting story that proves alluring to its editors, a fiction that seems to have materially changed on an editor's return to its pages. Was Steven Archer's story "Burrowing Creatures" formally symptomatic of its own concerns? I began to believe so. Sinking and rising, friendship and family, everything was beguilingly unstable by each turn of the evolving manuscript, to the point that I didn't know what to expect even as the story went from final proofs to the printed pages of a bound and stable *AGNI*. I wouldn't have been surprised if fog emanated from the last printed page. That "Burrowing Creatures" is a debut short story might be breathtaking if it weren't also a story that seems to have always been in the world, wholly confident in its strangeness, as inclined to inundation as it is to renewal.

Mary O'Donoghue, Senior Fiction Editor
AGNI

Burrowing Creatures

Steven Archer

BEFORE WE MOVED THROUGH THE RIFT, THE APART-
ment I lived in with Papi had walls of landlord white. I never
minded. The neighbor who sat me had white walls, too. On our
trips to the library, while Papi cut hair at the shop, she gave me
money to scan photos out of nature books, and I hung the black-
and-white printouts at home. The music Papi played when he came
home was a kind of paint—cumbias and ballads and folk tunes,
songs he said my mami had liked before she died and older songs
he'd heard on his parents' knees back in Peru. Those songs felt
orange to me. Like Papi's camotes, or dusk on a west-facing coast.
Like the beach photos he showed me of all the relatives he and
Mami had left behind.

He played the usual songs on the ride down Alligator Alley the
day he took me to see the property he'd bought. The exit to Cape
Coma wasn't even paved back then, the Gulf Coast rift so new.
First one discovered in Florida. What little I knew about them I
learned from Papi.

"Extra land," he explained. "*Magic* land, where anything you
bury will grow."

It was the summer before third grade. I dozed in my booster
that day, but Papi woke me to see the rift as it neared. It rippled
like two curtains off the side of the road, the seam where they

met glowing white. The two sides of the opening dragged over our windshield as we entered. The inside was car-wash colorful and just as noisy, loud enough to drown out our music. Beyond was a quilt of wide roads and build sites, the scrubgrass between them full of skinny trees and scorpions.

Papi took me to the place our house would go. Orange flags poked out of a weirdly symmetrical hill.

"Aquí ponemos tu cuarto," he said with his toe in the dirt, and the beginnings of a house rose just where he said, a maze of planks in the shape of a floor plan. We watched the house labor itself from the earth and I wondered what he'd buried to grow it, but only briefly, because the sun was setting, and Cape Coma had a west-facing coast, and the orange that settled across our hill and the grasses was the same orange I found in Papi's songs. I trusted it.

At the end of summer, when the house was all grown and our white apartment was packed and I'd swiped the library's nature documentary from the sitter, not knowing when I could borrow another, Papi and I moved in, and I was excited for the ways we might grow: dug from our old lives and planted like potato halves, slice-down and warted with eyes.

FOR THE LAST week of summer, I played alone. If I wasn't help-ing Papi clean the construction dust out of the corners and win-dowsills, I was rolling in the grass or spinning in the street while a second house assembled itself on a neighboring hill that I almost had to visor my eyes to see, like an explorer. I practiced burying things. I brushed dirt over my stack of library printouts and wa-tered the mound, and days later the same pages came up but in full color, and I pinned them to my walls. If I stayed still too long—reading on the lawn, or waiting for the bus—the Cape took it as a cue and did its best to copy me. I'd find an indent in the grass beside my own, the same size. On cool mornings, the fog studied my shape and mimicked it. That's the best it could do with people.

One day a boy stood in front of that second house, pivoting slowly with something held to his face. Whatever it was, he aimed it at me.

"Tenemos vesinos," Papi said that afternoon, folding my ear to make room for his clippers. My summer hair tufted onto our new kitchen floor.

"I saw one of them, I think," I said.

"Which one?"

"A boy."

"Did you say hello?"

I shook my head. Papi scolded me not to move. His voice and the motor echoed in the near-empty house, down to the corners of the rooms our old furniture felt too small in. "I met the boy's father. He is important here. He makes the business happen."

This meant little to me at the moment, a phrase so completely alien that my brain disregarded it as Papi went on to talk about school and the bus I'd catch in the morning, how the same boy would wait for me there, at his important father's instruction. And come Monday, there he was. The boy's name was Lucas. While we waited in currents of fog, he showed me the footage he'd shot of me that day from the front of his house. The camcorder, caged in his gnawed fingertips, looked glossy even in the hazy predawn light, and on the display my grainy face grew bigger as he zoomed in from his end of the street. Across from us, the fog arranged itself to match our silhouettes: his offered hands, my bent neck. On the bus, kids gawked over seat backs at the gadget Lucas held, and when he showed them my video and said, "Yeah, we're making a movie," the aperture of their favor widened to fit me as well.

I huddled close to him and asked, "*Are* we making a movie?" he said, "Do you want to?" and I said yes, and the matter was settled. He turned to film the passengers' fog-selves chasing the bus before the sun burned them away.

THE FIRST TIME I visited Lucas's house, all the baffling adult words Papi used about the father and his business took on a shape I could recognize, like seeing our doubles rise out of fog. The shape was this: They were people with money. As I got older and the rift economies boomed and collapsed on national TV, I'd learn how the right to bury came with the land, how some bought the land with loans, and what the banks meant by *foreclosure*. But that year, following my first new friend into his home, I learned all I needed from the living room alone.

"Pick something," Lucas said, sweeping his arm across the inset shelving around his family's TV. The long back of it disappeared into an alcove, like the house had grown around it. Disks and tapes lined the walls in crisp cases. Nothing familiar. At home we watched only what we could intercept on the antennas Papi made from paper clips and foil.

When I couldn't pick anything, Lucas chose a tape with a dirty word in the title, or so I thought. It turned out to be about a ship that sank. I thought we'd watch on his living room couch, but he took it instead to his bedroom to play on a second TV, ceiling-mounted with buckles and straps. He talked all the way through. I listened hungrily, about miniatures and sets and wrecks and submersibles, despite knowing so much already from my nature docs. When one character sketched another in a dimly lit room, Lucas paused it to place his fingers on the woman's stuttering VHS nipples, and this became only the second time I hid something from Papi, after stealing the documentary from the sitter. My second secret.

On my way out, Lucas's dad complimented my hair. It made me self-conscious. My fade played well on the southeastern coasts but felt finicky next to Lucas's blunted, shaggy bangs. At home a good cut hid that you were broke. Lucas didn't have to do that. All my former camouflage felt useless here.

"My dad cut it," I said.

"He told me he was good, but here's the proof. No wonder he wants to open a shop."

That world—our dads', of hands shaken and money exchanged, of contracts and loans—existed through a rift of its own, barred to my understanding by a curtain in the air, as unreachable as the home I'd left behind. I didn't yet know what drove people like him, drawn to the Cape not because his means carried better there, but because land so fresh sinkholed easily into pockets like his.

A FEW NIGHTS later, we buried Mami's earrings. The backyard stretched a ways, the limits of our lot delineated by tall amber wire-grass, punctuated with scrawny trees, and Papi crouched as close to the border as he could, scooping at the earth with one cupped hand. He dropped the jewelry into the hole like fat, pearlescent seeds and tamped over them.

I was taller than him when he knelt. The perspective felt wrong. His square hands, more familiar dirty than clean, stayed folded over the mound where I imagine he hoped Mami would grow— like the house he'd bought us, like the boy he'd moved into it, like the business he'd gone to Lucas's father about starting. The sky reddened fast overhead, a slapped cheek, and even when I noticed a disturbance moving closer, parting the grass in a slow, deliberate line, Papi would not lift his terracotta face to mine.

AT SCHOOL, SOME friends the camera bought us couldn't decide what game to make of the hole under the playground. They waved us under the plastic rock wall. Its topside was too hot to climb in the August sun, so we huddled in the cool beneath. A tyrannosaurus fossil was stamped into the plastic that curved over our heads and concealed us from the teachers. This was for the best— the hole was big enough to stick a hand into, but dark enough not to want to, and the threat of having our curiosity kneecapped by meddling adults made us zip our lips and drop imaginary keys into the black depths of the hole itself.

"This can be in my movie," Lucas said, fishing the camera from a bottomless cargo pocket. "Pretend you're looking for treasure."

The other boys were quick to task, crafting a make-believe about a cursed amulet and a dinosaur archaeologist who must have suffered some awful consequence.

"This must be where he started digging!" said one.

"What if it's booby-trapped?" said another.

"There's only one way to find out." The first lofted a piece of mulch toward the hole, and I broke my silence.

"What if it's a burrow?"

Lucas lowered the camera from his eye. "Dude, you ruined it."

"What kind of burrow?" the one with the mulch said. His name, I learned later, was Dean. I described what I could remember from the DVD, the one my sitter was probably accruing fines over from the library. I tried and failed to compare all the burrows I listed to this hole in the ground. Mole, armadillo, owl, gopher, gopher tortoise—Lucas perked up at that one, telling us how his dad complained about all the trouble they caused developers like him.

But Dean ignored him. "How do you know so much animal stuff?"

"I have this DVD," I said.

He asked if he could watch, and Lucas found another opening. "We can watch at my house. He has nothing to play them on."

It stung. But he paid for it. The boys that's-okayed him and went off to do something else. I went with him and watched, though, for myself more than Lucas's company. I missed the animals. I missed hearing the narrator's voice, the familiar musical cues, and I knew of no other way to conjure that comfort than to go to his glittering house.

At the end of an hour on burrowing creatures, with Lucas trying hard to seem uninterested, the narrator's use of *elusive* lit something in his mind, the challenge of a thing he couldn't see or have. The film—our film—Lucas decided, would be about the Cape's own burrows, the lives they concealed. Finding the animals. Discovering nests. I would've been thrilled, had he not used the word *hunt*.

———

ALL AROUND CAPE Coma, hills rose out of flat land and swelled until businesses split out of them—Walmart, Kohl's, Carrabba's—the way dragonflies burst from their own molted backs. Papi's shop was one of them. He buried his first pair of scissors to grow it, plus a loan from Lucas's dad. He came home happy, smelling like Barbicide and buoyed by borrowed money. The school year rolled on, August into September. We went shopping, had nice dinners, bought new clothes. We shrugged off Broward County like Mylar blankets, the flashy remains of a crisis. When he pulled out a seat and readied the clippers to shape up what hair I'd grown, I declined, and he looked hurt for only a moment. Every night, Papi watered the earrings. Every night, something stirred in the grass.

Eventually a hardware store opened, and Papi took me to choose paint colors. I hadn't even thought about painting. It had been forbidden at our old place.

He held up swatches in the light, while I clung to the front of a cart filled with stirrers and rollers and paint trays. He was taking the lead for most of the house, but I could pick any color for my room, and the choice was easy. I scanned the displays for my perfect orange.

Papi stared at it a while, then at me. "Your mami loved this color," he said. He held my hand while the shaker rattled our paints together, and at home we spent the afternoon moving things away from my walls and taping up the baseboards. This is how he found the DVD I'd stolen, pushed carelessly under the bed.

"Is this the one Mirta is looking for?" he asked. "De la biblioteca?"

I stared at his feet.

"Te estoy hablando."

Our eyes met. I nodded, and he crouched.

"We don't steal things, papito. We borrow. And we give back. Hm?" He waited for me to nod again and said he'd mail it back to her in the morning, once I wrote an apology to send with it.

He wiped the tears from my face and said we could keep painting my room if I promised not to steal ever again. I didn't know it was a lie when I said it.

The last things to clear away were the printouts pinned to the walls. I stacked them on my dresser, and my room became a sunset, one pass of the rollers at a time. Papi played his music loud. When the walls dried, I didn't hang the papers back up—they looked dull now against all that color. I set them aside, crumpled and pinholed, and when the Cape realized I'd discarded its gift, the bright inks fell from the pages as black dirt, leaving only the monochrome pages I'd first planted in the yard.

LUCAS COLLAPSED HIS first burrow on a field trip to the tidal flats. We padded onto the wet-cement sand in water shoes, smelling of sunscreen, stepping over veinlike streams and watching for crabholes—some of us more than others. Mangrove roots poked up from the muck ("knees," the guide told us, though they looked like fingers), and shorebirds prowled large among them like the chaperones among us, slow and long-legged, their arms arcing toward our worksheets like the curlews' long beaks. They split us into groups. I joined two girls from a different teacher's class, identifying worms and bivalves by their tunnels and mounds, marking each on my sheet, giving them human names, waving goodbye, and muttering to myself in the narrator's accent. Across the flats, Dean and the other kid—was his name Adam?—made sketches while Lucas dollied his camera low across the ground. He came to the picnic benches late, holding garbage in one fist. His lunch box hung heavy at his side.

"Hide my trash in your lunch box," Lucas said, dropping his sandwich bag and Capri-Sun on the table between us. The yellow straw showed like a spine in a vacuum-sucked body.

"Why?"

"I'll show you later."

And he did, on the bus, lifting the tin lid of his lunch box to reveal several pounds of sand and a hermit crab lying upended on the surface. I said, "What did you do?"

He said, "Not so loud!"

Adam perched over the seat back. "Show him," he said, and the camera came out of that bottomless pocket, and on the hinged display I saw Lucas crouching with his lunch box held open like jaws, biting a divot out of the wet gray sand that the tide would not smooth for hours, like the trenched fields into which our dads had sown trade. "I thought I could take his burrow with us," Lucas said, lying. His smile, the laugh Adam tried to hide, Dean's rolled eyes—they all blurred, my face hot. I thought of the tide rushing slow over the flats. The cool relief of night for all the hidden creatures—sea life marching shoreward with no birds or sun to fear. Had the crab been a mother? Did a crab-dad await her in the dark, wondering where she was? Would he find a portal and cross it to seek her? Had their child known her enough to miss her or would he follow without knowing why?

———

PAPI STAYED OUT late as the novelty of his shop wore off, hoping to draw working clientele with evening hours. At home, he practiced with scissors on busts from the toy aisle, cheap Barbie heads smiling under blond bangs. His clippers sat dormant. Barbering was different in the Cape, so many fine-haired heads patronizing his chair. In Broward, he'd been asked for by name.

I did homework in the backyard on his late days, the house too cavernous and empty. I laid my workbooks open in the grass, watching for scorpions, watching the sun comet toward the lot of tall wiregrass west of us. Every so often I'd arrange my limbs differently, to give the lawn a new shape to copy. Papi always returned before dark, in time to water the earrings. Except one day he didn't. The wiregrass pulled the sun into itself, like tentacles gathering prey, and still he wasn't home.

I filled a jug with the same smelly well water we bathed in. The odor was less offensive outdoors. I poured it over the spot where the earrings lay interred and watched as the wet soil began to give, sinking from the middle in collapsing rings, the earth swallowing itself until I was looking down into a depression the size of a salad bowl. Inside, white shapes sat dusted with soil, too large to be Mami's pearls. Mushroom caps, maybe? I blew on them, not wanting to touch. It was a clutch of eggs.

Sitting on my heels, I listened for the parting of the grass.

The floodlights clicked on, automatic, and I sat in a cone of yellow as a gopher tortoise emerged from the wiregrass, stony and huge.

She drew herself forward on powerful legs, the meaty curves of them studded with gravelly scales that shrank as they tessellated into her shell. Her wrinkled neck supported a waxy head, her almond eyes half lidded and glossy black. Her shell was wide, domed, caked in soil, big enough to sit on, bigger than my documentaries said this species should get. Had the Cape grown her that way, larger than life? Had she come for the earrings? Or from them? She drew near and aimed her back legs at the nest, moving more earth into place where my water had collapsed it. The eggs disappeared under the dirt. In another moment, she was gone, too. The grass parted for her. Her backside lumbered away in the dark. The porch door opened as the wiregrass stilled, and Papi found me outside, my hand extended toward her absence.

I ALMOST DIDN'T go when Lucas's birthday arrived, but his was the only house with a pool and Dean said he'd go if I did. So I went. It was the end of September. It always felt like summer in the Cape.

Papi wanted to send me with meat for the grill, as a courtesy to Lucas's dad, but then he said he was thinking anticuchos and I begged him to stop. I loved them, I did—skewered beef hearts in vinegar—but the last time he'd fed them to people my age, a girl in my kindergarten class asked what it was as she chewed, then let the morsel fall mangled from her mouth. I couldn't bear to watch that twice.

Lucas showed us the hermit crab while his dad cleaned the pool. She was still in the lunch box, the lid propped open over her shallow burrow, her bits of moldering fruit. He'd painted her shell. Even if she made it back, she'd be unrecognizable.

"Dad says they live longer as pets," Lucas said.

But was that well water he poured over the sand from a cup?

Was it even salted? The crab moved as he doused her, bubbles foaming at her strange little mouth. She'd be dead in no time, sick and weak until then, her armor reduced to ornament. His dad called us to the pool, where I sat with Dean on the edge, playing a dumb game.

"Nool poodle," Dean said. Sunlight caught in the dew on his face.

I answered, "Fool ploatie."

"You just copied a pool word!"

"Okay," I said. "Um, animals. Rackjabbit."

Dean considered. "Kermit hrab."

"Pemperor enguin."

"Topher gortoise."

Something fell into the soft earth of me then, a feeling for Dean I'd someday call my first crush. That's when Lucas's father's shadow scattered us. Dean went looking for a restroom while Lucas's dad sat down next to me, his feet plunging deep in the water. "Having fun, bud?"

I said yes.

"That's good. Your old man couldn't make it out, I see."

"He's at work. He wanted me to bring you food, but—"

"Oh, we've got plenty of that. No worries. But hey, would you do me a favor?" He waited for my attention. "Tell him to give me a call. Or better yet, to come see me. Can you do that?" His head eclipsed the sun, leaving a halo around his wet hair, his burned face. Free of his unthreatening polos and office palette, his body up close was scary, animal. Veined and furred. Ruddy where the sun had sat heavy on the shelves of his muscles. He made Papi look as small as a chess piece.

"I can't reach him is all. I'm sure he's very busy."

"Yeah."

"Try, though." He winked. "I'd really appreciate it."

There was a commotion behind us then, and every head on the whitewashed pool deck turned to see Lucas, pointing scared, calling for his dad, screaming about a spider descending from the pool screen. Like he'd done it a million times, his dad took the long lighter from the grill and immolated the thing in front of us. The silk burned instantly; the spider fell on fire, its legs curling like paper, the carcass whining with heat. "I hope you all like barbecue!" he said, stomping out the flame, and most of the pool deck laughed.

Dean found me again when the plates were passed, hot dogs and chips and Hug juice in little barrels. He said it was funny how afraid Lucas was of spiders, yet also obsessed with burrows, which some kinds of spiders are known to dig. I told him Lucas probably didn't know that. It wasn't in the documentary.

PAPI WORKED LATE with nothing to show. I couldn't find it in me to relay what Lucas's dad had said—not when Papi came home looking like he did, a deep-sea specimen out of his element, the whole of him air-pressured flat.

Dean and I spent our rotating specials period together, waiting each week that first half of October for our hour in the media center, when we could pore over high-gloss photos of the wildlife around us, the spreads wide enough to cover both our laps, cross-sectioned burrows coaxing us closer, swallowing us whole. We studied the gopher tortoise. We learned they're known to lay their eggs in a place separate from their actual burrow but close by, buried within reach. That would explain the yard, the grass. She must have had a home in the wiregrass field, queen of the empty lot. We learned that the latest the eggs would hatch was the end of November.

I told Dean about her then. He pinky-swore not to tell Lucas.

The bus rides grew quiet as my friendships shifted weight. Lucas didn't seem to notice—he'd gotten a handheld game for his birthday.

The fog kids at the stop stood farther apart every day. They didn't bother chasing.

On the playground, Dean and I watched from under the plastic rock wall, our backs to the tyrannosaurus fossil. The grooves of its bones nestled into the grooves of ours. Lucas would run past filming a game of tag, one eye to the viewfinder, the other squinted shut. When the teacher gathered us in from recess, she'd stop him to beg for caution.

"If you hit something holding that, you'll just hurt your own eye."

"I'll be careful," Lucas said. When she turned away, he stuck out his tongue.

Between my crossed legs and Dean's, the "booby-trapped" hole from that archaeologist game was occupied for the first time, a wolf spider's eyes staring wet in the shade, our threat to each other an impasse.

LINING THE MAJOR roads like carrion, shuttered businesses decomposed into the soil they'd sprung from. Papi's shop was among the first, an early casualty of the property bubble that I'd learn about as history once I could understand such things. But I was with him when he locked the door for the last time, and watched as the building disintegrated from the top down, as easily as a sandcastle. He walked into what was once the middle of the floor and swiped the dirt around until he found the scissors he'd buried. He wiped them off, pocketed them. They were all he'd ever get back from the site.

It was in this aftermath that Papi visited Lucas's dad. I stood by his side while he knocked. Lucas's dad ushered mine to his lair.

Lucas, in his room, ignored me, playing games while Papi initialed his terms of defeat, so when Lucas got up to pee without even looking at me, I pocketed the shell he still kept in that open lunch box, the sand in it dry, the paint on the shell flaking off, the body raptured away.

My father regained some of his shape after that.

A wholesale opened whose roots drank off half the businesses for miles. Papi worked for it gladly, making normal hours, coming home early enough to lie on his belly with me at dusk, the uneven ground of our yard pressure-pointing our fronts. This is how he met the tortoise: face down, level with her eyes. The grass delivered her right to his view. He fed her lettuce and berries, cleared debris off her nest. As October waned, we left her the scraps of our pumpkins and delighted as she pinched at the flesh. Papi smiled, serene. The same orange light that gilded her shell and scales lit the cracks in his face like mineral canyons. Like warm clay.

"It's her," he said. "She's telling us she's here."

But I wasn't convinced. Who was it who'd ventured from a good home, after all, for an open place to plant his child? Who was it who'd followed an instinct and wound up exposed, at the mercy and charity of others? How like a sun our floodlights must have looked through the wiregrass. How like the rift.

DEAN WAS WITH me when the clutch began to hatch. The surface of the nest warped like a thick stew as the hatchlings broke from their eggs, still buried, searching for light. We were side by side, waiting for the first to emerge, when Lucas called from the side of the house.

"You took my crab," he said, pointing at me. It had taken him weeks to notice. I would have said that, or told him it wasn't a crab anymore but a shell, but those would've been admissions.

"No I didn't."

"Yeah, right. I bet you have it there." Lucas eyed the soil at our feet and squinted, his mouth a confused parabola. "What is that?"

I tried to say it was nothing, but a hatchling had freed itself from the roil, small as our child palms, smooth and round. The Rorschach patterns on its shell glowed the yellow-green of nearly ripe bananas. It made its feeble paddle-path to the lip of the grass, which parted as it did for the mother, born to hidden in less than a minute. Lucas's shoulders sank, loose. His face softened. He walked the rest of the way up to us, looking straight at the nest, as if hooked by the bridge of his nose. He looked pacified, perhaps by the wonder of the scene—a climax for his film, what everything had been building to whether he knew it or not.

"Let me take one," he said. A look at my face, then Dean's. "You took my crab, I take a turtle. It's fair."

I shook my head. Dean said, "Not a chance."

"People will move in next door," Lucas said, nodding at the lot. "If I take one home, I'll be saving its life." He sat down between us, staring hard. The silence pulled taut. He could tell we wouldn't budge. I thought he might hit me. I wish he had. He lunged not at me but at the nest, not to grab but with his fists, smashing and grinding, three, four, five quick hits, a weak sixth as Dean threw him back by his collar, as I howled "Stop!," as black dirt sprayed the air. He scrambled away from Dean and stood, reaching his dirty hands into that bottomless pocket as Dean advanced.

Lucas joined the camera to his face like the siphon of some buried clam, filtering threat into evidence.

"Don't touch me!" he said. "Try something and I'll show my dad!"

Dean was predator-quick. He slammed the heel of his palm against the lens and Lucas screamed, the viewfinder entering his eye. He stumbled, wailing, clutching his face. The camera thudded to the grass. I scrambled to pick it up and eject the memory card the way I'd seen Lucas do, then pitched it into the field where another house was destined to grow.

Turning away while Dean wrestled Lucas out of the yard, I knelt again and spread my hands over the wreckage of the nest like I was testing for heat. The soil did not stir. I ran careful fingers through the gray, black, and brown, looking for babies, looking for eggs, but all I found were earrings, pearl-and-gold, struggling to shine.

CAPE COMA FILLED quickly, crowding by the day. New neighbors bought up the land between Lucas's house and mine until the wiregrass lot was the last open space. One final house rose up as forecasted, as though overnight, obscuring the sun long before it reached the grasses and blocking that particular orange light from ever touching our house. I never saw the tortoise again. Others would spill out of their fields, though, all across the Cape, unable to hibernate with their burrows collapsed. They'd overturn in our septic ditches, explode under tires on the roadsides. I'd think of those remains at night, in our next white apartment after we left the rift, but as I learned how to streamline my anecdotes about growing up there for friends at school, then in college, then at work, some of whom had grown up in other rifts, I mentioned the tortoises less and less.

The night before school started back after break, I buried what was left of the hermit crab in the ruins of the tortoise's nest. I buried it deep and smoothed the dirt flat. I wasn't sure what would happen, and didn't much care. Everything we'd planted since moving to that place had crumbled back to dust. I stopped visiting. Never watered the shell. Never waited for anything to grow.

Steven Archer is a Peruvian Haitian writer from South Florida. He holds an MFA from the University of Central Florida, where he was Provost Fellow in fiction, and is an alum of the Tin House autumn workshop. His work has appeared in *AGNI, Strange Horizons, Foglifter, Superstition Review,* and elsewhere.

Editor's Note

Samantha Barrett's "Invert" caught our attention from the very first sentence. What starts with some high school graduates near the beach buying beer with a fake ID turns into an exploration of queer identity and longing. A meteor shower serves as the perfect metaphor for the wondrous and the seemingly unobtainable—or rather, a failed meteor shower comes to symbolize the disappointments of life.

Throughout the protagonist's exploration of self and circumstance, Barrett weaves in wonderful prose that brings the story to a dreamlike level and enhances its intense moments. Even eating cherry tomatoes becomes something to behold. At the same time, the story grounds the reader in the reality of its sensory details and consequences, reminding us that life is precious and worthy of our attention from the mundane to the catastrophic. The piece comes full circle at the end, and the final sentence packs as hard of a punch as the first in this singular story of queer pain and beauty.

Milo Todd, Coeditor in Chief
Foglifter

Invert

Samantha Barrett

1.

THE FIRST TIME SOMEONE ASKS YOU TO HURT THEM you're eighteen. You're in that house by the beach, the place the five of you decided to rent for the single weekend this summer you could all see each other. Jeremy had to leave early, which means it's just Mara, Cassie, Logan, and you.

Up here everything is choked in mist. In the mornings, when you're outside on the shitty white plastic chairs that are already beginning to crack, you swear you can taste salt in the back of your throat. No one is particularly eager to go down to the water, a shared reticence for which you're quietly grateful. You've always been a poor swimmer. In middle school you had mandatory lessons: After the first one you would always deliberately misplace your bathing suit until the instructor got exhausted and let you run laps the rest of the year.

Today there's supposed to be a meteor shower, so you hop in the passenger seat of Logan's truck and you two drive down into town to buy booze. It's not as if your company is necessary, but being alone in the house with just Cassie and Mara only highlights how different you are than either of them. Besides, you enjoy watching Logan when he uses his fake. There's a poise about him that's almost theatrical. He exudes total belonging. The cashier barely even glances at the ID before taking the money.

Logan doesn't know this, but you have imagined his teeth on your skin. You have imagined what his hands might feel like against your nipples. You aren't certain if you're into boys or not, but you find it is easier to want them, defanged of the palpable disgust and self-loathing you feel for wanting to be with girls. Logan doesn't know a lot of things about you, but you like him anyway. Afterward you go out and lie in the truck bed and drink two of the beers. The bed is cold and moist. Your shirt clings to your back. The beer is barely enough to get you tipsy, which is unfortunate: You like being drunk. Often you feel it's the only time you're capable of speech. Logan asks what you're majoring in again and you say philosophy. Logan laughs and asks you what kind of jobs you're going to get with a philosophy degree. You don't know. You tell him so. You upend the bottle over your lips and wish it still had beer in it.

You ask him if you're ever going to see each other again. He thinks about this for a while. His face is between you and the sun and the light is making a corona of glowing mist around his head. He is so beautiful and you want to tell him but you don't say anything. He says maybe, yeah, ever is a long time. It's not what he means, but you're grateful for him saying it anyway.

You're about to pitch your empty bottle overhand into the empty parking lot when Logan stops you, says wait. He drives you halfway back up to the house and parks the car at a spot where a little cyst of green protrudes off the road up the bluff. A wooden fence circles the fringe of the overhang, strung together with rusty wire. You walk up to the edge and feel the siren-song of the drop. You imagine what it might be like to hit the ground, less the pain and death and more the tremendous, immediate *reshaping*, the body rendered in an instant into some anatomically impossible work of sculpture.

Logan dangles his bottle over the edge and lets it go. Two-thirds of the way to the ground it scrapes the bluff wall and instantly becomes a bright spray of sea glass. You hurl yours end-over-end. It describes a beautiful arc into the thrashing waves. Intellectually you know it was probably battered to pieces moments later, but you want to believe some sympathetic current caught it and pulled it out beyond the horizon to drift forever. You feel closer to Logan than you ever have or ever will again. You get in the car and drive back home.

At home Cassie is in the kitchen boiling pasta and cutting up radishes and cherry tomatoes. Mara is outside, reading something Baudelaire, her feet propped up on that big glass table that plays host to a nest of spiders. You're maybe a little bit in love with Mara but you try not to think about that. Instead, you spend a while helping out Cassie in the kitchen, an activity which pleases you both. You find something deeply satisfying about carrying out instructions, lending your hands to someone else's will. You put tomatoes in your mouth and split them beneath your teeth, feeling on your tongue the seeds still slimy with their caul of flesh.

When you're done cooking the room is hot and the sky outside is dimming. You and Cassie plate everything and she says thanks and you feel some small ember of pride flare inside you for a moment. You enjoy cooking even though you don't do it much. Once you cooked for Mara and Cassie and Cassie's then-boyfriend, Ethan. Ethan said you would have made a good housewife and you had to pretend you were fucked off about it instead of how you really felt, the tinge of red in your cheeks and ears. You don't believe that women's role is in the kitchen. You're a feminist, or at least as close as an eighteen-year-old boy can get. Even still, you often daydream of working over a stove, feeling someone's arm around your shoulder, their lips at your earlobe. You think maybe that makes you a bad person.

It's too hot to eat inside so you slide the dirty glass doors open and serve the pasta on the web-wreathed table. A spider crawls out from a crack in the metal and under the arch of your wrist.

You think about sealing it beneath the domed bottom of your beer bottle but by the time the thought arises you've already anthropomorphized it too much, made it a metaphor for yourself. You wonder if this is what getting older is like: everything loading itself up with symbols and meaning until you can barely move.

The light goes. For a moment the sky is apocalypse-orange, then the dull purple of a bruise. The four of you drink more beers. The empty bottles accumulate in the center of the table like a mass grave. You rest your chin on the table and stare at Mara through the glass of the bottles, the curvature catching and distorting her face into a confusion of flesh-toned blobs.

Full dark now. The sky is cloud-choked, an irregular gray-and-black canvas that catches and reflects the feeble light of the town below. You drag the chairs out onto the lawn and set your gaze heavenward. You're not certain how often the meteor shower occurs, and you're too far in to ask now. Is it every three years? Every twelve? Every century? You imagine yourself hurtling through the upper atmosphere, the air around you beginning to glow as your skin boils away. You envision the line you would draw in your brief, luminous existence. You feel warm. You drink a little more.

Has it started yet? You can't tell. Once you think you see a flash of light from behind the gray, but that could be anything: a distant stroke of lightning, the belly lights of some low-flying plane. You wait for a while. You drink more beer. Someone starts booing—Logan, maybe. The rest of you join in. You're booing and laughing and Cassie is yelling change the channel and you finish another bottle and then you have to go inside because the clouds are getting heavy and it looks like rain.

Halfway through the movie it starts pissing down. It roars against the glass, making the light from the town below blurry and indistinct. You're watching *Gladiator* because it's the first thing Logan saw in the cabinet under the house's TV and Logan bought the alcohol so you all owe him. You are drunk enough that your body seems to be slowly sinking down into the couch. The movie has become a blur of sensation, dissolving at the edges. Characters enter, monologue, die.

Cassie rises from her seat and staggers for a moment. She announces that she is going to bed, and you all moan about how she's a spoilsport but let her go. The three of you shuffle closer together to fill the space that she vacated. Through the queasy warmth of drunkenness you find yourself suddenly aware of the heat of bodies close to you, the press of their limbs, the pump of their blood.

The movie draws to a close. The beer has pooled in your limbs, leaving them leaden. You feel almost vegetative. Mara asks if you should watch another and you manage something like a yes. Light on her feet, she slides to the cabinet. You like to watch her move: smooth and graceful and utterly self-possessed, as if she were the undisputed lord and sovereign of each and every one of the trillions of cells within her body.

(Try not to think about Mara's body.)

She says: Oh fuck yeah. She spins and turns to you, hugging a Blu-ray to her chest. By moonlight her face and arms are almost porcelain-white. Her face reminds you of a Noh mask you once saw in an art class: a blank canvas, features penciled in black and red. You realize you are tremendously afraid of something but you don't know what.

Caligari, Mara says. Us three, right now. Logan groans and gets all pissy about watching a movie that *doesn't even have COLOR, for chrissakes*, but he folds without much convincing. Logan is a good guy, even though he thinks he's a pit bull. He is the nicest boy you know, and he will stay that way until five years from now, when he flips his car while veering to avoid a deer and then very quickly afterward he will stop being anything at all.

You are watching the movie. You expected it to be incomprehensible: It's German, nearly a century old, and you're drunk besides. You're more drawn to it than you expected. You're reading the images more than the dialogue—deep blacks and harsh whites, cities leaning in on each other like a closing jaw, murder and madness.

You are drawn to the man inside the box. Maybe "man" isn't right. He's a weapon, a ghoul the doctor conjures up to bloody his hands for him. At times he seems less like a person and more like a part of the architecture. You watch him kill and abduct. When he is carrying away his quarry it is like he and she are made of opposite matter: she, white and almost glowing, he of ink-darkness. You feel like crying. You don't know why.

After a while Logan yawns and stretches. He looks at you with catlike indignancy and says sorry guys I don't really do this artsy shit. He gets up and you both tell him goodnight and he says goodnight you two and then he gives you a look that you don't understand but you don't think you like and then he is gone and you and Mara are alone.

She slides up on the couch so that your bodies are touching, and you let her even though you're pretty certain if she keeps touching you're going to vomit. She is maybe the most terrifying thing you have ever seen. You wonder if it's somehow objectifying her to be this afraid, to invest in her this much power. Right now you think she could probably destroy you with a word, snap your neck with a wave of her hand. Part of you wishes she would.

The movie is still going, but every part of you is focused on her body pressed against yours, the heat of her bleeding into you, and you have to place every quantum of your being where you two meet because otherwise you'll catch on fire or explode. Your body is betraying you and you loathe it, loathe every part of it, from the no-space between your legs to the wires that spring from your chin. You want Mara to put a cattle stunner to your head like in *No Country for Old Men* and kill you.

She looks up at you. Her eyes are so big and she is so beautiful. You pig. You fucking swine. You don't deserve this. You are thinking about dying when Mara says do you think I'm pretty and you say yes of course I do how could I not and then she grabs your head between her hands and drags herself forward and then she kisses you.

She breaks off the kiss and then she grabs you by the shirt and she kisses you again and you are totally empty all hollowed out inside like a bodhisattva and she is guiding your hands toward the soft warmth of her body and she kisses you again and her hands

are up your shirt writhing like twin serpents against your chest
and she is saying off and you are obeying like the dog you are, like
the nothing you are, you are nothing except what she wants you to
be, and she is taking off her shirt and you see the subtleties of her
body and she is sliding off her bra and a part of you wants to slit
your wrist to the elbow because she is so impossibly beautiful, she
is the most perfect thing you have ever seen, and your body is an
affront to Heaven, an unclean thing, larva on a god's corpse, and
you will never ever ever be the slightest fucking thing like her you
tranny cunt and she is saying ███████ do you want to fuck me
and in that moment you cannot imagine wanting anything more,
would fuck her instead of food instead of water instead of oxygen
because she wants you and all you are is a tool a body to be used
and she is unzipping your jeans now and you are letting her and
you are terrible down there and she says do you have a condom but
you don't so she gets one and slides it over and her fingers touching
it are the most agonizing thing you've ever felt like a hot iron brand
but then she straddles you and slides on top of you and then you
are fucking her, watching yourself fuck her, because this isn't your
body, because you're not really here, because you've never been a
human being at all, and she says choke me and you do, squeezing
sides not esophagus, playacting a murder, and she says harder and
you squeeze a little harder and she says harder and you squeeze a
little harder and she says fucking harder and you don't do anything
and then she hits you.

Your senses briefly disconnect. Your cheek ignites with pain.
For a single instant, you choke her, your thumbs crushing her
throat, and then you are pulling yourself away, feeling like a monster, feeling like a rapist, feeling like they haven't yet built the circle

of Hell to which you deserve to be condemned. Fuck, Mara says. I'm sorry, you weren't responding and I just.

You are sitting on the couch not saying anything. You are watching yourself sit on the couch saying nothing. You are screaming fucking say something freak and the other you is sitting on the couch saying nothing.

She says ██████?

She says ██████ please say something and so you say I'm okay I'm sorry.

She says I just wanted to make you mad enough to choke me for real and you say I understand. You are thinking about werewolves and monsters in human skin and torches and pitchforks. I should have just done it you say.

It's fine she says. ██████ don't worry about it.

You are putting on your clothes. She is putting on her clothes. She is unreachable. Her light is cast by a dead star.

I'm going to go to bed, she says. Are you okay?

Yes, you lie.

The two of you hold there for a moment, like actors waiting for their lines.

You say: I'm sorry I didn't.

It's fine, she says. Really, it's alright. I promise.

She stares at you for a while. Eventually she leaves, slipping back into her private darkness and closing the door behind her. You curl up on the couch.

Tomorrow, when you wake wearing a veil of sweat and a jackhammer hangover, this will not have happened. It will have been excised from the record, film cut and spliced. You should feel grateful about this.

Instead you feel numb. You will wake up feeling numb. You will drive home still feeling numb. You will feel nothing at all for the next two days, and then the pain will all come down at once like a thunderbolt and you will scream and sob and drink an entire bottle of Jack Daniel's and try to castrate yourself with a carving knife and get yourself sent to the hospital and when you go back to school you and your parents will agree to pretend your appendix burst so no one has to know what kind of creature their "son" really is.

2.

You don't learn Logan is dead until three days after it happens. You are lying in your bed laboring under the sickly heat of a hangover, feeling your stomach writhe its many protests. When your phone buzzes you have to peel it from where it's been wedged between your body and your mattress. *I'm sorry about what happened to Logan. I know you were close.*

You put the phone on your desk, strip yourself nude, and wander into your en suite. Two slender shoots of fungus are growing from between the tiles in the corner. You turn on the shower and the water bangs and rattles in the walls and comes down in a great tongue of fire. You close your eyes and feel it run against your skin until you're certain when you open them your flesh will be running off your body in pinkish rivulets, deconstructing you down to the bone. Something racks you. A sob rattles against the tile-and-glass cubicle.

You get out and dry yourself. You allow your hands to settle in the places where hormones have softened you. It's not enough: When you stare in the mirror you can still feel that old static at the fringes of your vision.

You change your clothes and then you pick up your phone and look at the message again. *I'm sorry about what happened to Logan. I know you were close.*

And you don't need to read anything else, because you know what Happened, know that it was the last thing to ever Happen to Logan ever again. God's eyelash fluttered in Their sleep and broke his body and drowned him in his own blood and set his beautiful face in a death-rictus until the worms came to tear it apart.

I'm sorry about what happened to Logan. I know you were close.

The room is suddenly unbearably stifling so you make yourself some approximation of presentable and head out into the street. Outside it is bright and hot. The air is soupy, swamp-like. The clouds hang low enough that they seem poised to crush the top floors of penthouses into powder beneath their weight. People huddle for cover beneath the shade of overhangs and scaffolding of endless construction. After only a few minutes of walking you're already wiping away the pearls of sweat that settle in your eyebrows.

You're not going anywhere in particular. For the moment your room is unbearable, too coffin-like in its silent confines. Even being alone among people is better than being alone in there, where you sometimes lie on your bed in the dark and find you can't tell whether you're awake or dreaming, high or sober, alive or dead. Every shoulder that collides with yours, every body that pushes past your own is another reminder that you're still separate from the sleepers under the ground.

You are trying to align Logan's life with your own, to slot the moments of his death into your own hazy memory of the night it happened. He was on the West Coast, so you factor in a time difference of three hours. For some reason the moment *it occurred* is deeply important to you, as if a superluminal transmission burst from him the instant his vitals failed and flipped a switch in your brain that changed everything forever. When you were dancing in a blackout haze, was he winding his car through forest switch-backs? When she cornered you against a wall, kissing until you were desperate for breath, did he already have some impression of what awaited him? When her hands were pulling your hair, the cherry of her cigarette searing constellations into the small of your back, had the metal and glass of the car already redefined his anatomy?

You want to reach out. Logan had parents, a girlfriend, now mourning alone somewhere. Do they remember you? You doubt it. Even if they did, you have a different name now, a different-enough face. Your own strangeness would trouble their memory of him, an irreconcilable element.

Fuck, you need a cig. Your hands are performing their little St. Vitus' dance. You're supposed to have quit but you duck into the next bodega you see and buy a pack anyway. There's a photo on the back of a woman exhaling smoke through a hole in her larynx. The image has never bothered you before, but now it makes your stomach churn.

You find the nearest bus station and hitch a ride down to the city's edge. Out here the accumulated heat of a couple million bodies all boils off into the blue. The bus drops you off near a sunbaked concrete platform jutting out over the bay. There's a railing separating you from the water, and you lean on it, peeling the flaky white paint from the metal with your fingernails. The smell coming off the sea is heady and richly organic. You imagine a rotting corpse, and then Logan's face surges up in your mind's eye and you feel sick.

You produce the cigarettes, perform your ritual pat-down. An image flashes in your mind's eye, infuriating in its clarity: a half-empty red lighter, partially obscured by the other garbage in your trash can. You flick the inside of your wrist, hard. The momentary pain realigns your senses.

You don't want to go home so you just stand there for a while, the wind biting at your neck, your forearms jittering like the needle on a seismometer. People come and go. Seagulls pull half a gyro from a trash can and tear at it like hyenas picking apart a carcass.

Eventually a guy comes and lights a cigarette. You descend upon him like a bird of prey. You modulate your voice a little, a note brighter, a pinch breathier.

Hey, you say. Can I borrow your lighter?

Yeah, he says, and extends it held between his forefingers. The wrapping is dollar-print. Benjamin Franklin stares up at you impassively as you light and inhale. You expel a tight little cone of smoke that spills apart into empty air.

Thanks, you say. Up close you have a better look. The guy (not quite a boy, you think, but not quite a man either) is handsome in that soft, unassuming kind of way. He could be twenty or twenty-eight. The patchy scruff of an attempted beard clings to his face.

I'm Travis, he says. He's a little shorter than you, enough that he has to look up to meet your eye. He has this kind of lost-puppy feel to him and you can't tell if you find it attractive or off-putting. Vivian, you say. That's a pretty name, he says, and you just nod and take another drag on the cigarette because you really don't want to talk about your name, not while he's standing this close. You are running little risk-assessment subroutines in your mind, each result only bifurcating into further questions: *does he know, if he knows, does he care, if he cares, does he want to fuck me, if he wants to fuck me* and down and down and down it goes.

A moment of quiet. You tap out ash on the railing and the sea wind flicks it sailing miles out. There's some great mechanical drama occurring a half mile or so down the waterfront: A bridge is folding itself up to admit a huge container ship ponderously slicing down the canal. Travis jabs his cigarette toward it. I work on those, he says.

You blink. Fuck, he's a—stevedore? Longshoreman? Do they still even need those? You don't know, and you tell Travis as much. He laughs.

Not that kind of "work on," he says. I program navigation algorithms. Well, technically I'm in the beta branch of the team that programs navigation algorithms for ships above a set tonnage on behalf of a company that's part of a conglomerate of companies that own 21 percent of global shipping.

You roll your eyes in mock exasperation. Lord, you say. Save me from this plague of coders. Travis clutches his chest like he's been dealt a mortal wound.

You tell him about your job running translation for the American wing of a tech company based in Stuttgart. He asks you for some German and you tell him that he is too skinny and that the wolves will eat him soon, and then you tell him again in English.

Jawohl, meine freunde, he says. His accent is abysmal. When you leave you have his number written on the see-through skin of an unwrapped cig, and you fold the paper carefully into quarters and put it in your breast pocket and prepare to never think about Travis again for as long as you live.

Your shift doesn't start until 3:00 a.m. local so you hop a train up to the tourist neighborhood. It was (so you're told) an artist's colony, until gentrification caught it in its death grip and turned it into a theater for the endless reenactment of its former self. The city has sliced up the elevated rail and turned a portion of it into an elevated garden.

You climb the switchback staircase with a paper container of chicken and rice clutched to your breast like an infant. Nearby, a group of women are taking turns photographing each other with their phones in the dying light. In places like this you enjoy pretending you're some tumorous cell, some quantum of infection that's slipped into the inner chambers of power. It's more exciting than being a lonely girl eating her dinner (or breakfast, depending) alone in the high wind.

You call Cassie. You don't know you're doing it until you've already tapped the call button and wedged the phone between your chin and shoulder. The phone rings for a long time, and you imagine yourself inside some immense stone chamber, the noise echoing out, only to be met by its own distorted reflection.

A woman says Hello?

Hi, you say. Is Cassie there?

No response. Through a hiss of interference, you can hear the contours of another voice. Is there someone else?

Who is this? she says. Her voice is clipped, guarded. How do you know my name? Um, you say. The wind bites your skin. A discarded bottle of kombucha rolls under the guardrails and shatters

against the street two stories below. Someone curses. A car alarm
begins to wail. Wait, she says. Holy shit, ████████?

It takes a moment to register that she's talking about you. The
boy that name belongs to is dead and buried. It's only by coincidence that you share the same body.

It's Vivian now, you say. But. Yeah.

Wow, she says. I—hold on. You hear her putting the phone
down, her voice intermingling with another woman's. Sorry, she
says. A friend.

I heard about Logan, you say. I'm sorry.

For what?

What happened.

Oh, she says. Oh my god, yeah, it's terrible. To be honest,
though, I'm surprised you care about that.

Of course I care, you say. He was my friend.

She doesn't say anything for a while after that. You imagine
the phone resting on the table, Cassie hunched over it like a di-
viner over a scrying mirror, some faceless other standing attendant.
Well, she says. She speaks slowly, as if you are a child. When you
left we thought you didn't want anything to do with us.

Later, back at home, you pack a bowl with the last of your weed
and go smoke out on the balcony. The sun's death-rattle is turning
the sky beautiful colors. You feel like the smoke and the twilight
and the clouds are all becoming a single substance, the same substance as your body, and if you pulled yourself over the rusty railing you could drift across the rooftops forever.

Down below the vital pump of the city keeps flowing. Before
you moved here you'd dreamed of The City as a kind of platonic

aspect, a self-sustaining machine of energy and culture and life. You imagined yourself dipping into its veins like a mosquito, engorging yourself on the pneuma of this place. You were foolish. It is possible, you have learned, to be surrounded by the teem of life and yet touch none of it.

Later you lie in bed and scroll Grindr. The images are mostly torsos: torsos rippling with muscle, slender, girlish torsos, torsos broad and girded with layers of fat. You saw a scientific exhibition of skinless human bodies when you were twelve, and something in the arrangement of today's pickings reminds you of the same. You imagine flayed forms grinning up at you, their bodies held together with something more akin to jerky than flesh.

Your phone buzzes. You've got a match. Username: h3ll_h0le. The guy is huge: a broad chest, a heavy gut, thick arms capped with dark hair. An arrowhead of fur stretches up toward his belly button. The image leaves little to the imagination.

h3ll_h0le: U horny

jeanne.belladonna: yeah

Another image: the rest of his anatomy. You feel something warm in your gut at his size.

h3ll_h0le: U like?

jeanne.belladonna: i do

h3ll_h0le: U want me to hurt u

h3ll_h0le: whore

jeanne.belladonna: i bet you could hurt me

h3ll_h0le: let me see you

h3ll_h0le: be my little porn star

jeanne.belladonna: getting hot for you daddy

You spend a few minutes adjusting the lighting in the room before stripping your top off and baring your tits to the camera. You look away, affecting a coquettish reluctance. On the screen your skin looks so very pale, a maggoty white expanse.

h3ll_h0le: hot

h3ll_h0le: i wanna cum in u

jeanne.belladonna: what else do you want to do to me

h3ll_h0le: i want 2 put my hands on ur neck

h3ll_h0le: i want to squeeze

h3ll_h0le: i want u to beg me for air like the little faggot whore u r

He sends you something else but you can't read it because suddenly it has become very difficult to breathe. The world swings drunkenly. Your vision is a blur of deceitful colors—whites, reds, blacks. You feel your vise-grip on the phone loosen, hear it clatter to the floor under the artillery barrage of your own heartbeat. You gasp and it feels like your lungs are about to pop.

You lie there for a while, drawing ragged gulps of air, listening to your blood thunder in your eardrums. Where are you? Not in your body, or at least not in all of it. You feel vacated. You are weighed down by strange meat. Where did all this flesh come from? You fire impulses down strange channels and a five-legged white spider flexes before your face. You feel queasy.

After a while you come to reinhabit yourself. You watch your ceiling fan slice the air to shreds in the dark. The sheets cling to your sweaty flesh as you roll from your bed and paw beneath it for your phone. h3ll_h0le has sent you something else but you block him without even reading it.

Your body is still unfulfilled. It's not even lust anymore. You cannot escape the conviction that you are beginning to disintegrate, that you are slowly becoming something other than matter. You have dreams of staring in the mirror and watching a rash of nothing crawl down your shoulder, flesh transfigured into something like ectoplasm that splits and falls away at your touch. Something deep in your gut insists that if your body is not held soon it will cease to exist at all.

Travis. His boyish features stare up out of your phone. He's not unattractive, you have to admit. You imagine his slender hands brushing against your hips and a pleasant shudder courses through you. When you like his profile you match immediately.

FTbeowulf: heyy girl! fancy seeing you here!

jeanne.belladonna: hey

FTbeowulf: until i saw u on here I would've never guessed u were TS lol

jeanne.belladonna: haha

jeanne.belladonna: thanks

FTbeowulf: do you dance?

Impressions: darkness, drunkenness, heat. Your body gyrating beneath throbbing purple light. Eyes on your flesh, tracing the slow crawl of sweat across the pale expanse of your exposed skin. You know what it's like to be lusted after. The power it gives is ephemeral, but you enjoy holding it when you can.

jeanne.belladonna: a little :)

The club where you meet is called Bateau Ivre. Outside, a neon sign affixed to a scaffold depicts two frames of a cartoon sailboat with a hole busted in its side. You're wearing a black dress with the back cut off. Before you left you stared into the mirror, moving your arms, watching the skin distort beneath the wide expanse of your back and shoulders. Whatever is in your gloss is making your lips tingle.

You force the door open and the club exhales a hot breath out into the night. Inside, the DJ is grafting a Lil Wayne verse onto a Smashing Pumpkins melody. The dance floor is a thicket of limbs; seaweed stirred by ocean currents.

You take a seat at the bar, order a negroni (wincing at the price), and spend the next few minutes making it disappear. Someone drives an elbow into your back and you slosh gin across the surface of the bar. You turn and meet the gaze of a short girl wearing a hot pink jumpsuit. She scans your face, and when you lock eyes you are struck dumb by what you find there: a bright, fearsome dart of loathing. For an instant, you are frozen, locked beneath her withering gaze.

She relaxes. Her expression assumes a doelike placidity. She waves her martini glass and a little splashes on your dress.

Slaaaaay, she drawls. Her friends pull her away. Their bodies lose coherence, becoming detached limbs, floating torsos drifting in a drunken fog.

You pull your phone from its secret pocket along your bra. Travis says *sorry! running late- 10m.* The bartender's cloth slashes across the table, and another cocktail is placed in front of you. You look at the bartender. He says: From the man at the other end of the bar.

You lean out. A wide, bearded face grins at you. As soon as his gaze meets yours he slides off his stool and sidles toward you, affecting a cowboy swagger.

Hey, babe, he says.

Hey, you say, not meeting his gaze, trying to put up all your defenses. You are thinking: *Not me. Someone else. Go away.*

Y'wanna dance, he says. You could take a lighter to his breath. You are trying to compare his frame to yours. You're the same height, but he must have fifty, seventy pounds on you. That's sweet, you say, but I can't. I'm waiting for a friend.

He whines. It's a strange sound, higher and thinner than you would've expected. Does he store it in some secret bladder underneath all that flesh?

Come on, sweetheart, he says. Don't be like that. You are reaching out in your mind, searching for the exits. How fast could you push through this crowd, if you had to?

Really, you say. I'm fine.

His big hand tightens around your shoulder, and you whirl at him, hands clenched, nails poised to cut.

You drop your voice as low as it'll go. Fuck off, you say.

Confusion touches him, then horror, then contempt. He squeezes your shoulder as hard as he can, and then just as you're about to fling your drink into his face he releases his grip. Fuck, he says. Fucking faggot. He flicks his hand like he's trying to dislodge snot. He stumbles into the crowd.

You take your negroni and slam it. That familiar poisonous warmth. Your oldest friend comforts you. When Travis shows up you don't even really speak to him. You clasp your hands around his wrists like manacles, drag him spinning out onto the dance floor. You circle each other, a terminal orbit. You want to taste his sweat, draw his being into subordination with your own. In the bathroom you kiss him until you're gasping for breath, and when he drags his hand down the front of your dress you can only barely tell him *no, not yet.*

You stagger back to his apartment. When you leave you half expect to see the man from earlier waiting outside, accompanied with friends and bottles, but outside it's just the night and the cold. When you get back he puts on something by The Weeknd and makes you a gin and tonic. You put it down slowly, staring at the New California Republic flag on one of his walls.

When he sits next to you on the couch you kiss, casual and unhurried. His hands trace over your body without quite touching. You can taste the gin soaked into his tongue as it probes the unfamiliar terrain of your mouth.

Fuck, he says. I've never, he says. Been with.

You're a virgin, you say, and he shakes his head.

No, he says. I've been with girls, just never with a. Even if I've imagined it a lot. You nod. Obliteration, your old companion, is crawling back into you from your fingertips upward. In a few minutes this won't even be your body anymore.

You kiss him again. His fingertips trail down the side of your dress, smoothing out the ripples. His hands move inward along your thigh, but no further.

Do you still, he says. Do you have—

I have a penis, you say. You curl your hands, and let your nails bite into his back. He lets out a pleased little moan.

What do you want, you say. What do you want. Tell me.

I want you, he says. You drive your nails in a little deeper. I want *you.*

To do what.

Destroy me, he gasps. I want you to destroy me.

I can do that, you say. For the first time you really believe it. You are going to hurt this man the way he wants to be hurt. You are going to bleed annihilation. You are not a girl, you are a window yawning wide. A black wind blows through you. You are going to unmake him.

To the bedroom, you say. Obedient as a puppy, he goes. You wait for a while, slurping at the watery dregs of your drink, and then you strip off your dress and walk into Travis's bedroom and do your very best to hurt him.

You succeed beyond your wildest expectations.

Samantha Barrett is a trans woman from the California Bay Area. She currently attends Bard College in New York. This is her first published work.

Editors' Note

brandon brown's "Faultline" grabbed us immediately. It was breathless, beautiful, and rhythmic. It threw us right into a place and time that was familiar (evening, parking lot, a group of slightly menacing boys near a field and some dark woods) but askew in a way that made the story keep expanding and surprising. The conditionality of the sentences, the reuse of the "if" made us feel like we were being led down a path that was ever-splitting, and each move forward in a direction felt precarious and exciting. It is an aching, lovely, painful, and perfectly written story about self, about remaking, understanding, growing, and coming together in quiet and electric moments when *being* briefly supersedes caring about how to be.

Amy Stuber and Maureen Langloss, Editors
Split Lip Magazine

Faultline

brandon brown

IF IT IS A WINTRY THURSDAY NIGHT. IF THERE IS A
football field and players and a wilting ball. If the same old boys
are smoking out on the field's edge. If there is a black dry forest,
and out of the forest's dark mouth winds a dirt path, and the dirt
path passes the field. If Avery, on the way home from her job at
the pub, emerges from the forest and follows the path. If a fizzling
streetlamp struggles to light the path. If in the lamp's sorry light
Avery glimpses a figure among the boys at the edge of the football field. If it is Sam. If Sam has always seemed lost to her. If the
years have slipped by since she last saw Sam. If she's spent years
circling a question she can't voice. If she feels like she's seeing Sam
for the first time: soft and strong, brilliant and gold. If she has
heard rumors about Sam, how they keep company with the football boys. If she remembers Sam's high school boyfriend. If she remembers blowing Sam's high school boyfriend in the locker room
and thinking of Sam the whole time. If the lamp's light is sorry, but
Sam is smiling at her. If she could have been a painter, a botanist,
somehow alluring. If she feels like she never had a choice. If the
players out on the field follow a plan, a plan she has never been able
to understand or access. If Sam's smile lifts her. If Sam asks, "Do
you want a smoke?" and Avery says, "Hell yes." If there is a hunger

in the cold air between them. If the boys kick the dirt, caught
in the failing lamplight with Sam and Avery, made small by the
enormity of the field and its rules. If the boys, watching from the
sidelines, eagerly track the ball, the players, the state of the field.
If the boys believe they have made a choice to live by the field's
rules. If there is comfort and stability in living that way. If there is
pain in it, too. If the boys yearn for victory but fear they are in the
midst of a lie. If Avery asks what Sam does for work and they say,
"I'm a carpenter—I made these," and they flick the gauges in their
ears. If harsh smoke fills Avery's chest. If she coughs and hacks. If
they gravely say, "Smoking's bad for you," and lead her toward their
car, away from the boys. If Avery says, "Sorry," and she's talking
about the locker-room blow job. If their hand on her shoulder, firm
and calloused, is intoxicating. If they sit in the driver's seat and
she sits on the passenger side. If Sam mumbles sorry about the
boys. If Sam says, "I feel like I pass when I'm with them." If Avery
wishes she could soak up the shame. If the winter has been long
and strange. If they kiss. If she invites Sam to the back seat of the
car, and they squeeze through the thin slot between the seats, the
oily light warping the shadows, the ratty back seat sinking beneath
their dirty sneakers and cold asses. If Sam was her friend once. If
they reach for her cheek and trace her neck, and their fingers slide
across her collarbone. If her breath catches. If she has dreamed of
this. If she has kept a ledger. If the ledger counts all the ways Sam
might have touched her and never did. If she kisses Sam again. If
it is hard and pleasant and eerie. If she wishes she might change—
might erode, might *bloom*—the way Sam has. If she guides Sam's
hand to her spine. If she presses their finger against a groove in her
skin. If she says, "Here." If they do. If they rub a finger along the

groove, sink their nail into the skin, and finally begin to peel her. If Avery has always wanted to ask what else can she be. If she makes a wish. If she is a rippling curtain. If she is a golem. If she is a cloud. If she is the soil clinging to their sneakers. If she is stark, breathless entropy. If Avery unfurls, and if the groove is a knot in who Avery is, may be, can never be again, and her skin sloughs off, lying on the back seat like folded linens. If this is a faultline, an opportunity— if Sam plunges their freckled face into Avery's neck and sucks in air, and they breathe of a meadow teeming with skin and hair and ferns, of the forest, if, after all this, Sam exhales winter: the football game is lost. Sorrow grips the boys. They howl out on the field's edge. They rap their knuckles on the car's rear bumper, oblivious to what has happened inside. They brawl and hug, bruised, defeated, fumbling their way on the dirt path and into the dark mouth of the forest. In the car, Avery is in Sam's arms, cracked open against the leather seat, a human figure, a rift of possibility. She's the car's yellow overhead light. She is the forest. The football flying. The cigarette smoke in her lungs, too, or the lungs' agitated tissue. The world's hers. She wraps her arms around Sam. Her hot breath mingles with theirs in the quiet. Now, what else can she be?

---

brandon brown holds an MFA in writing from Vermont College of Fine Arts—what they call their "MFA in strange stories." They're hard at work on a novel of linked stories about a Southern town besieged by climate change and eroded reality. They grew up in upstate South Carolina and now live in Albuquerque, New Mexico, with Felix, their loudmouth cat.

Editor's Note

Sammi Chiyao's "Corn Soup" asks a compelling question: How do you handle your mother's release from prison? And, what's more, how do you live under the same roof with her holding the knowledge that she did, in fact, commit the act for which she was incarcerated? Throughout, the relationship between the mother and daughter is electric with tension as they navigate the change in their dynamic, the shifting balance of caretaking and control as the narrator tries to help her mother reenter a world that "tastes sharp without the salt of other people's breath." A world that has moved on without them, but that still remembers, still judges. Chiyao, in prose that is tight, deft, and controlled, forces us to look closely at this complex familial landscape that interrogates what we owe one another.

Wendy Wallace, Editor
Peatsmoke Journal

Corn Soup

Sammi Chiyao

BY THE TIME I SPUTTERED INTO THE LOT, MAMA WAS on the curb shivering, arms curled around a plastic bag of her belongings. She'd been released that morning, but I was late only because I was reluctant to scrape the ice from my windshield. She came unhurried to the car. When I asked her why she didn't wait inside, she said that the air out here tasted sharp without the salt of other people's breath.

Mama's probation counselor advised me to acclimatize her gently: familiar places, familiar foods. Seeing as how Baba wasn't around anymore to make her favorites, I took her to the dim sum place near our old apartment. Mama washed our chopsticks in cups of watered-down pu'erh, her neck straight and sun-spotted hands dignified as if she hadn't spent the past seven years with plastic sporks too soft to cut skin. We gorged ourselves on lo bak go and cheung fun until the trolley lady scowled at us for calling her over too many times. "Don't get used to this," I warned her when I saw her eyeing the mango pudding. "This is a one-time-only thing."

That mango pudding was the last thing we splurged on. Mama knew about our financial situation, of course, but she was too overwhelmed in those weeks to come up with any ways out of the hole. She couldn't even comprehend her release requirements. She sat there smiling dumbly while her counselor listed them out: not only did she have all the usual probation meetings and drug tests, and their fees, but she had her restitution payments—and somehow had to find gainful employment with a seven-year resume gap. Plus, she couldn't drive, on account of her license expiring while she was inside. To her credit, Mama was polite when the counselor chewed her out for not yet applying to any jobs. She said sure, I'll just find a place that'll let me work half days so I can come pee in a cup here twice a week. They'll definitely go for it if I mention I'm a felon. All that in her accent still thick after thirty years in America, so I think the officer only heard the agreement and not the sarcasm.

Though I had my own reservations about Mama, I took pity on her when the officer threatened to send her back inside for a late payment. At the time, I was bagging at the big-box supermarket and worked so many holidays that my manager loved me. I cashed in my one favor to get an interview for Mama. Her English wasn't strong enough to sell herself, so we went in together. The manager let us sit in the creaky swivel chairs in the back office while he read through her application.

"Work history looks good," he said. "Twenty years at this handyman joint?" He ran his finger along the job titles I'd listed out: scheduling, accounting, customer satisfaction.

"Family business," I clarified. When Mama and Baba moved here, Baba took on any odd repair work; Mama, who grew up comfortable before her father frittered away their wealth, never learned any useful skills besides her calligraphy. She had spent all her years here appeasing impatient clients and entering Baba's jobs in a thick, leather-bound book that she never let any of us touch. I don't know if she ever aspired to anything else, before she realized that money could come far easier through the gaps in her miscalculated accounts.

"Back on the job market again?" the manager asked. "No problem. We get a lot of older folks in here, looking for a second-chance job." He hummed vacantly as he paged through the forms.

When he got to the end, he stopped abruptly. He looked at Mama. Mama spun around and around on the chair, legs dangling.

"Hey, I think there's a mistake here."

"Where?"

"Here, in criminal history," he whisper-yelled. He turned the paper around to show me.

I fiddled with the lever on my chair, reluctant to look at it. "No. That's right."

He hesitated, mouth stutter-stopped on his next sentence. Mama's face rotated past. I couldn't tell if she was acting clueless, or if she had receded back into her daydreams, unbothered by her future. Was she embarrassed that her mistakes were laid out in those checkboxes for all to see?

"She's nonviolent. And she'll work twice as hard as the high schoolers," I said. I reminded him the calendar was still short for next week. I knew he couldn't afford to turn away an employee— he begged me for double shifts nearly every weekend.

He stuffed the forms behind his cabinet as if to erase Mama's record from his memory. "She can work the self-checkout. Not the registers."

Mama started work the next day. Her job was easy enough, just to help out whenever the register threw an error, but she was jumpy around the customers. I think she never understood how they could self-scan when last week she couldn't take a shit without permission. I watched her from my aisle in case she needed help. Even if she yelped when a register started blaring, no one glanced at her.

Sometimes, Mama talked about prison. She brought it up at random and without fanfare, like when she made corn soup on our two-burner stove and told me about her friend Ximena who taught her this recipe, who came to the city with her two kids and three of her sister's. Or we would drive past a Jersey Mike's after her drug test, and she would say that Aggie swore her first meal would be their buffalo chicken cheesesteak when she got out. She said those women were her first real friends. I let her talk. She probably needed to convince herself that it wasn't seven years wasted. Really, I felt for her; it must've been lonely with only fleeting comfort from our visits each week, when Baba and I yammered on about the mundanities of our world as if she were still outside with us. But now we were free, and we could do anything she wanted.

When Mama brought up visiting, though, I put my foot down. It wasn't good to keep ties with them. You never know how those relationships turn out in the real world, when you're no longer on equal ground. Mama agreed, mostly because she had no other choice. I controlled the car and the finances. Between her probation officer and me, she couldn't take a step without either of us signing off on it, and it probably rankled her to no end. She didn't bring it up again, though, just put her head down and kept working hard at the supermarket like she told me to do when I was a kid.

———

WHEN I FINALLY dragged Mama to the salon, Mrs. Lau took one look at her matted hair and sat us in the back next to Yee Chong, the cashier at the market next door. I was heartened to see Yee Chong—Baba used to take me to his market after school, and he always let me pick out a melon candy from his bowl. I guess that was a long time ago now, since Yee Chong turned away from us when we approached, no sign of recognition. Baba was the only one of us who was good at keeping friends. When Mama went inside, I started doing the shopping myself so Baba could pick up more work, and I preferred the Walmart Supercenter where none of the cashiers would see me and think of Mama.

Mama sat mutely while Mrs. Lau and I chatted in Cantonese about her new Volvo and the unseasonably late snows. Then Mrs. Lau pointed her comb at Mama. "What do you want?"

Mama answered in English, each syllable deliberately crisp. "Give it a trim."

Mrs. Lau, undaunted, countered again in Cantonese. "You'll need more than a trim to fix that mess."

Mama hunched, the cape shriveling around her shoulders. "Make it quick."

I didn't know what Mama's problem was. She knew Mrs. Lau before everything, when they first moved to this town with Kowloon air caught in their throats, when Baba went to Mrs. Lau's basement studio every month for a new repair. Before my arrival gobbled up all their attention, Baba and Mama had Mrs. Lau and her husband over for dinner each week, and they would play cards and smoke Baba's counterfeit cigars late into the night. I thought Mama would embrace her friend, but here she was shrinking from her touch. I tried to catch Mama's eye in the mirror to silently admonish her. Her face was screwed into a knot of wrinkles.

Mrs. Lau set upon Mama's tangles. With every scrape of the comb against her skin, Mama flinched away wild-eyed until Mrs. Lau grabbed her head. "Stay still." I reached over for Mama's hand and she squeezed me so hard her nails left crescents on my palm. Mr. Kwok came over for Yee Chong's haircut. He started to complain about Yee Chong's dandruff, but when he saw Mrs. Lau ripping a knot through Mama's hair, he wordlessly turned on the clippers. Yee Chong's eyes flickered over to Mama, so tense she was nearly vibrating. I watched disgust and pity ripple across his face.

When I looked more closely at Mrs. Lau, I noticed how she held herself as far away from Mama as she could. Now I understood why Mama's animosity sprang vicious and unbidden. It was the same reason Mrs. Lau switched to another handyman after the conviction and, I realized now, why she would rush through our haircuts with mumbled excuses every time Baba and I came in. I faced Mrs. Lau, willing her to look at me, but she and Mr. Kwok carried on about the kids from the high school who went to juvie as if we weren't there. I stood from my seat. "Can you be gentler with her?"

"And use less water," Mama added.

"Speak Cantonese, honey," Mrs. Lau told her. To me, she tutted, "These knots aren't coming undone." With an exaggerated flourish, she brought the blade flush against Mama's neck and cut the knot clean off.

I was still fuming when we left the salon. "I can't believe

them. Mrs. Lau told me she was so happy you were getting out. She couldn't even be pleasant for one haircut. I thought you were friends. I babysat her daughter."

Mama fingered the choppy bob skirting her ears. "I'm not surprised. She doesn't want to feel like she owes you anything. Hurting someone is easier than being responsible for them."

I eyed Mama, suddenly irritated by her flippancy. "Was that it? You didn't want to be responsible for me and Baba anymore?" Until he died, I had hidden Mama's worst betrayals from him, her forged invoices and her manipulated affection, because I didn't want him to see what I saw. It was a blessing that he never understood the trial well enough to know that Mama had meant every error in his hard-earned accounts. "What would Baba say to that?"

"Baba doesn't need to approve everything I do," Mama said. She got in the car.

I stayed outside, gulping mouthfuls of air into my tightening lungs. For years after Mama went inside, I kept tabs on her victims. Most were destroyed by the debt, which had ballooned into something grotesque before they noticed—after all, Mama had a unique talent for sniffing out the ones who were the worst with money. Of course she never thought about them. It was impossible to make her understand her wrongs, and there was no point in it now that we were the only ones left. Neither one of us would survive my honesty. I ground my heel into a beetle on the pavement. Through the dirt-smeared window, Mama looked like she was made of glass. I got in the car.

On the way home, I asked Mama, "Did you forget your Cantonese?" She shook her head. "In English, in prison, I'm like everyone else—a nobody. But if I speak their language, I'm trying to belong with them. Why would I do that?"

MAMA'S FRIEND XIMENA got released the week after. Mama was so happy, I think she would've skipped all the way to the prison if I didn't stop her. Her stories of Ximena slid into fable: Ximena could identify your sickness with one touch, Ximena could transform a few expired cans into dinner for all five kids or four hungry women. When Mama was on janitorial duty, Ximena smuggled a bottle of vinegar from the kitchen to dissolve the limescale on the toilets. "To her, everything was useful," Mama said. "Baba would've loved her." I didn't get why she was all that great. She would never make Mama's tea right or know the perfect memory to comfort her when Baba came up. She was a temporary friend to ease the ache. Mama had me now—wasn't that enough?

Mama waited weeks by the phone for Ximena's call, but it never came, not even after I saw her out stocking shelves at Rite Aid. I watched Mama unplug and replug the Wi-Fi for an entire afternoon until I finally broke it to her that it wasn't happening. Mama sagged a bit, but she puffed herself back up quick, claiming Ximena was swamped with all her kids and her treatment program. Ximena didn't have it easy like her, with me taking care of everything. Secretly, I was relieved that Ximena must've realized she and Mama didn't have all that much in common on the outside. Now Mama would see she already had all she needed.

I was restocking the candy and magazines next to Mama one evening when this woman walked up. She wore the pinched confidence of a regular; I wouldn't have paid her any mind, except for Mama's fingers tightening around her clipboard when she approached a self-checkout register.

I would've missed it if I wasn't already watching so intently. She scanned some peaches and kale, straight into the bag. Then the king crab. Unscanned. She was smooth about it, practiced, as if this two-hundred-dollar purchase had glided direct to her purse many times before. Mama's eyes popped open. She started forward, a shout ready, but I clamped my hand tight on her arm. Never confront, all of our employee trainings had said. Don't accuse. It's not worth the danger or, more importantly, the disturbance to other customers.

The woman didn't even notice us. She walked past with her nose in the air and her free king crab in her giant purse, too good for the nobody cashiers in the bright red aprons.

Mama wheeled around on me as soon as she flounced out. "Why'd you let her go?"

"You wanna lose your job? You'd be fired if you caused a scene there."

"But she was stealing." I could see the bloodlust in Mama's eyes, already picturing that woman in her former cell. "I saw it."

In some ways, Mama had been sheltered during her time in prison. She hadn't yet realized she could get punished ten times over, but this woman could come in here every week to help herself to the free seafood buffet and we would still thank her for coming. "You already know how it'd go," I said, not unkindly. "Who's the manager gonna believe, you or her?"

"You would back me up. Two against one."

"I'm always on your side," I agreed. "But even if all the evidence is there, you'll never get him to listen to you."

Mama had no response. She stormed out the doors with her clipboard in hand, arm cocked back as if to pummel someone with the produce codes. The woman was stowing her spoils in her trunk. Mama headed straight toward her, and I winced, already dreading our manager's anger, but then she sailed right by her. "Where are you going?" I called. Mama kept going, down the block, across the next, through the Dollar General plaza. By the time I caught up with her, we were both wheezing. Mama shoved her clipboard into my hands. She headed for the Rite Aid on the other side of the next lot. I understood. Ximena worked there.

Ximena was by the medication shelves at the back, barricaded by crates of tampon boxes and heartburn pills. Mama plucked a box from the top so she could jab her finger directly at Ximena. "Why didn't you call?"

Ximena's eyes crawled from Mama's fingertip up to her face, ruddy and slick with exertion. If she was surprised by Mama's ambush, she didn't show it. "I've been busy." Her words came out carved in granite.

"You said you'd show me how to plant those chilies when we got out."

"We said a lot of things." Ximena shooed Mama away, but when Mama caught her wrist, she hissed, "When I met you, you were so small, like you didn't know how to exist without your husband to take care of you." She spat out *husband* like a swear word. "We knew you didn't belong there. I took pity on you, tried to give you something to hold on for. They were words. Now we're free. We're free. I have responsibilities, things to do, I have my boys, and my damn sister's boys too"—she waved wildly to the corner, where a few teenage boys sat slumped on the floor, phones in hand—"and you think I have time to play in the dirt like a kid? You need to grow up. You can't hide from your life forever."

Mama turned the tampon box over and over in her hands. I glared at Ximena's blackened nails, her bruised forearms, that self-satisfied frown.

"My manager's gonna be pissed—he's already mad I brought the boys here. I have to get back to work. Get out of here. Don't come around again." Ximena twisted away from us, hands furiously shelving the rest of the pill bottles.

Mama stiffened and walked down the aisle. She looked like a cardboard cutout of herself. I didn't know if I could make her feel better, so I said nothing. I shadowed her quietly, back around the lot, through the Dollar General plaza, across and down the blocks to the supermarket. No one had noticed our absence. The customers were still dutifully scanning their groceries, paying for them in full with the bag fee, streaming out of the store without a glance at us. I went back to my silent post. When nine o'clock hit, I wiped down my station, logged out of my register, and Mama and I crossed the darkened asphalt to our car.

Back when Mama was no more than the handyman's wife, she relished how everyone's eyes slid right over her. No one would remember her long enough to trace those unexplained bank transfers back to her. And if a customer ever came to our doorstep about an inflated bill, Baba's apologies—so earnest because even he couldn't see Mama's cunning—would always appease them. Now, though, I wondered if Mama still savored her invisibility. Maybe she didn't notice it anymore.

Something occurred to me. "You were watching that woman before—how did you know she was going to steal?"

Mama's voice was rheumy from hours without use. "People always have a certain look on their face when they know they're about to screw you over. I saw it in the guards inside, and in our manager when he realized I'd never complain about my missing overtime pay . . . A little delight, a little pity. Like they can't believe how weak you are."

WHEN WE GOT home the next day, Mama asked me to drive her to Rite Aid. I gaped at her. "You want to go back?" She shrugged. "She doesn't want to see you," I said. Mama didn't bother to argue. She just snatched up her bus card and some of our TV dinners and went outside to the stop. I watched her through the window. When the bus departed, I drove over to Rite Aid. Mama walked up a little while later and went inside. She came out after ten minutes, alone, shoulders sagging and hands empty.

Mama didn't ask me the day after. As soon as we got home, she took her bus card out the door, this time with the pot of congee she had made that morning. Again, I followed her. Again, she left with that same forlorn expression. But she didn't stop. A week passed, and she kept at it, doggedly trekking out to that Rite Aid day after day with enough food to feed the whole block. I don't know what she expected. Ximena seemed pretty clear the first time. Part of me pitied her hopefulness, but the other part felt an almost vengeful satisfaction: Soon enough Mama would realize that she could only move forward in time, not backward, and she would learn to be content with what we had.

Mama was inside for a while the next time. I waited in the

car, stomach rumbling, about to give up and drive home when she finally came out. Ximena was beside her. They were laughing about something. Mama shoved Ximena's shoulder, and Ximena snatched the ice cream from Mama's hand to take a bite. Where did she get that? I'd never seen her eat those before. Ximena's sons, or maybe her sister's sons, followed sullen-faced and gravel-kicking. They headed to the street, looking like a family from behind. Just before they turned out of sight, Mama glanced over her shoulder and I saw a strange expression on her face, as if she had left something important back at that Rite Aid. I started the car and drove off. I don't know if she saw me.

The next morning, I hid her bus card in my wallet. Then I emptied the box of cash above the fridge for good measure.

Mama was unusually chipper on our way to work. She was reminiscing about that zoo she and Baba took me to as a kid, the one with free admission on Tuesday mornings. She would always run off to score free tickets for the bird show while Baba walked me through the park. "We should go back there," she said. "I wonder if the peregrine is still around." I knew she was trying to make me feel better now that she'd won. I told her the peregrine died last year from the bird flu that spread through the enclosures during a cold snap. It spent its entire life in that cage and never got to see the forests five miles away. "Even so," Mama continued as if she hadn't heard me, "we should go back." She was still fixated on that zoo when I picked her up from her probation appointment in the evening, prattling on about the monkeys and the tigers as she went into the apartment. She hunted around in the catchall dish for her bus card. Her words died in her mouth.

"Have you seen my card?"

"No," I said. I turned on the television, set to whatever American reality show Mama was watching before work.

"I swear I left it right here." I heard the clanging of keys, and then a booming thud as the coatrack toppled over.

I watched Mama feel around inside the box atop the fridge. She withdrew her hand with a frown and then headed for the couch. I pinned my eyes to the television as she felt along the seams of the couch cushions, turning up a stray nickel and dime in her search. She asked me to get up. I stood, legs weakened with dread, but she unearthed only a few rusted pennies. Not nearly enough. I plopped back down in relief.

"Do you have money for the bus?" Mama asked me.

I shook my head, unwilling to lie out loud, and turned to the screen in hopes that Mama would finally lay this to rest. But she went through the nightstand in our room and the kitchen drawers, practically trembling in her need to get on that bus.

I turned down the volume. "It's no use. You're wasting your time with Ximena. She doesn't care about you."

Mama came to the living room. She stood in front of the television, her head barely clearing the top of the screen, her hands clenched at her sides. "Are you serious? Why are you doing this to me? No, don't look at me like that—like everyone else. Haven't I suffered enough?"

Mama knew exactly how to make me feel sorry. I was tired of coddling her. "You have to make up for your mistakes," I insisted. "You can't just run away to Ximena. She's not your friend."

"They weren't mistakes. I did them for us." Outside, a car backfired, and Mama turned toward the sound. It was too dark to see her face, but in silhouette, her profile looked bright and cold. "We had nothing. You know, people used to respect my family. I know what it feels like. And then we came here, and no one even looked at us when we took care of their shit-clogged toilets for half price. It was only a little bit off the top at first. You needed a new coat, or books for school . . . You were so young, but already you realized you were different from your friends. I couldn't bear it. What kind of daughter has to throw away her life to take care of her mother?"

The hard plastic of the remote dug into my fist. "Don't turn this on me. I never asked for anything. I just wanted you around." Mama was right. I was too young when she made her choices. How could I be blamed for what she did? All at once, I felt like a kid again, desperate for Mama to come home. My voice rose to a trembling scream. "I can't believe I defended you to everyone. I thought you would never jeopardize this family. But you were guilty. You must've always been guilty, your whole life, if you jumped at this as soon as you got the chance."

"I'm not the guilty one," Mama protested. "What about our customers, who made Baba work for free if they didn't like his first repair? They rejoiced in our weakness, all of them. These people will spit you out if you don't jump first."

Mama's words didn't even register. It was too late for her sob stories. "Do you even feel bad for those people you stole from? You ruined their lives," I said. "You ruined ours, too."

"Baba said they got the money back—"

"He was lying!" I cried. "That's all this family does, lie to each other. I lied to him for years. That you were doing the right thing. That he would see your release. And how did that end? He died with your lies on his lips."

Behind Mama, a contestant on the television got voted out, and she started crying; huge, racking sobs rippled through her raw-boned frame. Mama crossed to the window with such ferocity that I thought she would jump out. But she settled her hands onto the frame with a world-weary sigh.

My anger could snap Mama in half from here. The words flew out before I remembered why I never told her the truth. "I'm glad he died before you got out. So he wouldn't see how little you care about us."

Mama's entire body crumpled. She couldn't look at me. She just walked out. Even in that moment, I knew that my honesty—or was it cruelty?—had ruined something for good.

MAMA DIDN'T SPEAK to me for months after. I told myself I didn't care. I had spent years without her around—what was another couple months on top of that? In all of Baba and Mama's visions for their life here, the one thing Mama and I accomplished was our persistence, even if it left us alone in the end.

It was hard to pull off in complete silence, but Mama and I managed to get on with our lives: I helped her get her license back, so she could drive herself to her appointments; she got promoted to a human checkout cashier; I started working for Mrs. Lau at the salon for some extra cash. Mama's need to see Ximena vanished. In one weak moment, I showed her our empty bottle of painkillers to ask her to pick up more from Rite Aid. She wasn't excited at the thought of going anymore. GET IT YOURSELF, she wrote on the back of an envelope. I'M TIRED. I guess she realized that Ximena didn't care about her now that Mama had stopped chasing her down. Despite her best efforts, she was turning into a respectable woman, one that Mrs. Lau would seat at the front of the salon. I should've been happy. Somehow, though, everything she did seemed wooden, as if she had left all her conviction back in that Rite Aid parking lot.

I couldn't stop thinking about the day she got arrested. Baba told me that Mama was special because she loved her family more than she feared everyone else. He wished he could do the same. Back then I thought he was deluded by his belief in Mama's innocence, but I think his opinions wouldn't have changed even if he knew the truth. When Mama and I went at each other's throats during that first phone call, he said that this was what we were meant to do, as a family.

I was walking to the bus stop from the salon—Mama had the car that day for an appointment—when I decided to take a detour. It was pleasantly warm that day. The first flowers had forced their way out of the frost-hardened ground, and business was slow enough that Mrs. Lau let me off early. She handed me an envelope on my way out. Your tips for the week, she said, but the envelope felt weighty enough that I suspected she felt bad about Mama's haircut. I swung the envelope around in my hand as I walked. There was probably enough in here to replace the wipers on the car, or maybe even to repair our dishwasher. Mama would be happy about that one.

On a whim, I detoured by Dollar General to walk past Ximena's Rite Aid. I was thinking about that corn soup that Ximena made with Mama, and wondering how Ximena got corn in prison, and realizing that whatever she traded for that corn was probably pretty valuable but she must've thought it was worth it to comfort

Mama with one decent meal. Mama made me film her making it in our kitchen like she was a celebrity chef, and I cheered as her loyal audience. The soup itself was alright, hearty and warming, if a little bland for my taste. I let Mama finish off nearly the whole pot. She said that when she and Ximena made it that first time, on the floor of the commissary at midnight, she felt as though Baba and I were right there with her, crowding around for a taste.

Ximena's kids were outside by the dumpsters smashing glass bottles against the pavement. Some white lady got out of her car and yelled at them, and then stormed away with her phone out to call the cops. The boys frantically biked across the lot. They ran inside the Dollar General, their bikes scattered by the accessible parking sign out front.

I followed them to the entrance. Through the window, I saw them wandering through the aisles, five brown boys who made the Dollar General employees instantly stiffen up. I wondered if Ximena had anyone else to help her, like when Mrs. Lau came by every week with some fish stew after Mama first got arrested and everyone still thought she was innocent. One of the boys picked up a pool noodle shaped like a caterpillar. He swung it around, clearly delighted, until his brother came by and smacked him on the back of the head. He reluctantly put it back in the bin.

I turned away. The bus was coming soon, and I wanted to start dinner before Mama got too hungry. Behind the Rite Aid, Ximena crouched against the wall smoking, and she gave me a nod when I walked past. Just a little one. The sun was in her eyes, so she couldn't see my expression, but she squinted at me as if she knew exactly what sickness was afflicting me. As my bus arrived, I ran back and handed her the envelope of cash. She accepted it with the wariness of someone who expects nothing.

"I'm Kailing's daughter," I told her.

"I know," she said. That was all. Maybe another day she would come to our stoop with a meal of her own, or maybe she'd continue on without us. Today, at least, I hoped she felt my gratitude.

At home, Mama was watching her reality shows. I apologized for coming home without dinner. She didn't seem surprised that I was finally speaking to her, but maybe she heard something in my tone, because she looked up at me with unusual warmth. I hadn't noticed her smile lines before. When I asked her how her appointment went, she shrugged without saying anything, but she scooted over on the couch to make room for me.

Sammi Chiyao is a PhD candidate at Stanford University originally from Boston. She has received support from Kundiman, the Napa Valley Writer's Conference, and Seventh Wave and is an incoming workshop participant at Tin House. She is currently writing her first novel.

Editor's Note

"Elastic" is driven by the voice of teenaged Ryann, a dancer we meet in a hospital bed. Smart, sardonic, shell-shocked, her voice is just wise enough to barely disguise her pain. Ryann doesn't know if she will survive her Rare Condition, and neither do we. As her world narrows to daily trips to interventional radiology, jokes about foods she can't eat, homework that doesn't matter, and doctors that may be hot behind their masks (but does that matter either?), we get the feeling that maybe Ryann, the former one, has not survived, and we are hearing instead from a new Ryann entirely. This Ryann has learned to say goodbye—to dreams, friends, her strong body, that body's privacy, and her ability to make choices about it. Still, the ending surprises. It isn't just that death comes for us, but its terrible truths that we won't want to forget.

Jill Stukenberg, Coeditor
Midwest Review

Elastic

Joanna Demkiewicz

Sunday

I AM SIXTEEN AND HAVE BEEN TOLD NOT TO WORRY.
The nurse Tracy explains how to use the morphine button. I simply
press. Pressing the button feels like playing god. It's red like Red
Delicious and catches slightly every time I press. *Click–k.* Absence
of pain.

Tracy tells me to call her when I need to use the bedpan. To call
her, I press another button. My hands are free for button pushing,
otherwise I am completely immobile, with four IVs anchoring me
to the floor of the intensive care unit. My left arm is the Main
Event. It's wrapped in gauze and elevated onto a side table next to
my bed. My hospital gown is as thin as an eyelid, and my nipples
poke out like finger guns. This is my new look, and as I've always
been taught, you have to work with what you have.

I am told that I am at a teaching hospital, which means that
baby-faced doctors-in-training randomly invade my corner. They
look like they are my age, like they just put on a costume and messy
hair. But I know they are smarter than me. They have a purpose in
life. Each time they barge in, the doctor ushers everyone around
my bed, and they discuss My Rare Condition. If Tracy is checking
my IVs, she is asked to leave; there's not enough room. Some of the
students ask questions. Many of them are thrown off by my age.
"You're the best-looking patient in the ICU!" more than a couple

tell me, like we are old friends. One of them tells me we have the same name. "Ryann," she says slowly, pointing to her chest like she is speaking to a chimpanzee, or a baby. Eventually they always shuffle off, and I follow their voices to the next patient, and the next room, until I can hear only the beeping from my heart monitor. The thing is, I haven't been able to look in a mirror.

Tracy tells me I'm on a "liquid diet" because of all the drugs I'm on. We play a game where I ask if a particular food item is on the menu.

"Hamburger."

"Nope."

"SpaghettiOs."

"I don't think so."

"What about . . . marshmallows."

Tracy's eyebrows squish. "I'll have to check."

I ask Tracy what she eats, and I'm confused about her hours. "When do you leave work?" I ask, after she tells me her favorite flavor of the hospital cafeteria Jell-O is cherry. She says she has twelve-hour shifts. Sometimes after a shift, she'll walk across the highway to Just Nailz and get her acrylics touched up, and then fall asleep in the chair while getting her feet done. I imagine the women there placing a blanket across her chest after her chin bobs to her sternum. I ask her when was the last time she did that. She says last week. I ask her what color her toes are. She says Georgia Peach.

When my mom comes during visiting hours, I ask her to bring nail polish next time.

"Kiss Kiss Bang Bang, I think it's called," I tell her. "Okay," she says, but I can tell that she won't. My nails are bare because of my upcoming dance recital—no color on our fingers or toes is allowed, even nude. I realize, now, that I will not be there, because I missed rehearsal yesterday, and I will miss tomorrow, too. This means I can decorate myself with fire.

My mom has recently checked into the Ronald McDonald House, and her face is oily, slippery. Her boss has let her take all of her vacation time at once so she can be close to me, instead of driving back and forth. She grabs my free hand and tells me about her new temporary home. There are "no clowns" and she has housemates—other families with terminally ill or critically sick children. It's fifteen dollars a night per guest. Someone made eggs and bacon this morning in the shared kitchen area, and one mother did yoga in the common room. My mom says that she tried to relax but instead walked the exterior of the hospital four or five times, she can't remember. Then she tells me that my oldest friend Beatrix is visiting on Wednesday. I realize—

"How long will I be here?" I ask.

My mom pauses, poker face. She tells me, and I nod. The TV is playing reruns of old shows. Barbara Eden is asking her Master what he would like for supper. Her eyelashes are cartoonishly long, longer than any performance lashes I've ever worn. My mom is telling me about the actor Larry Hagman who plays astronaut Major Tony Nelson, and how he retaliated against blasé scripts by showing up on set in a gorilla costume. We laugh. Then she tells me that one day, while shooting a scene for the first season, the director quietly excused everyone off the set while Barbara Eden was locked inside an oversized perfume bottle. He idled in silence, waiting for her to realize that she had been abandoned, and then he recorded her screaming for help. He used the audio of her screams in another episode, *so authentic.* My mom tells me this and then shifts in her chair to a new position: her wrists joining each other in embrace, a feline with crossed paws.

It doesn't take much effort for me to fall asleep without warning. I think it must be the morphine.

Monday

Dr. Bishop is like the supposed victim of a snipe hunt: invisible. I don't see him, I am only reminded of our initial meeting in the emergency room before I was admitted into the intensive care unit. Dr. Bishop is a vascular surgeon, his office in another orbit. The only doctors I see are the ones in rotation, the ones who cart around eager students in scrubs.

Tracy is wearing blue eyeshadow today, and she is asking me a lot of questions. I notice that I can answer a question, but I don't always remember what the question was once I've finished my response. Memory is like trying to capture a cloud and convince someone nearby that it looks like a lion in profile, no a helicopter, no a bouquet of cauliflower. Tracy asks me what I am smiling about, and I tell her that I'm actually in a lot of pain, but that it's far away, like an itch that you try to resolve by digging harder into your skin. There's no point of contact for you to touch the itch to make it disappear. Tracy reminds me about the button.

It's official: When my mom comes during visiting hours today, she calls my dance coach Mary on her cell so we can explain why I won't be in the recital. I insist on telling her myself. I don't feel it coming, but I cry as I tell Mary this, or I think I'm crying because my face is wet and my mom looks very sad at me. I've never spoken to Mary on the phone, and she sounds younger, less harried. She tells me that my understudy Stephanie has been practicing her triple pirouettes and she's confident the solo will be lovely. Then she asks if Stephanie could use my headwear since I won't need it this year.

"If we order the crown for her now, it'll never arrive in time," she says. "You don't mind, yeah?"

"I don't—" I say. My mom slips the phone from my fingers, takes it off speaker and finishes the conversation in the hallway.

I don't think my crown will fit on Stephanie's head, simply because her hair is bigger, thick like a helmet. I don't think her triple pirouettes cause a glare like mine do. I don't think she gets her neck around in time to make it a perfect spin. I don't think she thinks about her body the way I do mid-pirouette, which is to say I imagine it expanding, taking up space, instead of what Mary tells us to imagine, which is that we are contained. I don't think I explained my situation correctly to Mary just now—*so, there's this intruder inside of me, and it could destroy me.*

Wednesday

I am told that I have been in this bed for longer than three days. I try to count sunsets and sunrises backward and then I laugh. *There are no windows!* Tracy asks why I'm laughing and I tell her. She laughs with me, and then we're both in on the joke.

Of course it's been more than three days. Yesterday after my mom left, Tracy and two other nurses changed my bedsheets for the first time, and I experienced the limit to morphine. I'm not allowed to be removed from my bed, so they changed the sheets as I lay there. The two other nurses cooed and shushed while carefully rocking my body to the left side as Tracy pulled the fitted sheets from under me and replaced them with starchy white ones, jostling me slightly as she worked. The nurse with the bowl cut was only gently holding my right calf as Tracy yanked on the bottom part of the bed, and my foot and ankle followed the dirty sheets as she removed them, I thought *for good*, I thought *goodbye, foot!* Pain distorts clarity, I realized, after it was too late, after I'd already slipped outside of myself, joining the mobbing crows above my head. I became only what I felt. I was, for a long moment, only Pain. After this, I slept for a very long time.

Dr. Bishop will operate on me in a few days. But in preparation, I am wheeled to another floor of the hospital, the interventional radiology unit, where I am operated on every day.

These trips widen the lens of my world. We go in an elevator. We pass a receptionist named Janet. We roll down long hallways where people in sneakers are walking to their appointments. Depending on timing, we sometimes pause next to a floor-length window, which looks out into the hospital's main garden. We do this today and catcall the electric blue cornflowers and the big-lipped peonies, pink and vulnerable like an animal's belly.

These surgeries are "minor" and so I am conscious during them. The doctors wear masks. I never see their faces, but I'm convinced today that the main doctor in green is hot. His skin is tan and smooth like wax paper. He tells me he missed me, and then he and a masked nurse banter. I think this procedure takes an hour, but I don't know. There is an anesthesiologist sitting on a stool next to me, talking to me and asking me if I feel anything. I imagine she manipulates my anesthesia like a movie pilot in a set-designed cockpit, inexplicably flipping levers and switches. I spend my time on the brink of consciousness, washing in and out of myself, focusing on the pimply ceiling and the ghosts tugging on my arm. It's over before anyone says, "It's almost over." I hear the masked doctors update Tracy on their progress. Something about "shifting the stent," something about the "implant in my subclavian vein."

On the way back to the ICU, Tracy and I play our game.

"Corn dogs."

"Nope."

"Red Lobster."

"Ha!"

"Butter."

"Actually . . ."

When we return to my room, visiting hours are about to begin. I now have a roommate, Robert, a farmer who suffocated in a grain bin but was pulled out and flown to the hospital by emergency responders. When Robert's family visits, they speak to him in loud, intentional sentences. He is in a coma. His brother doubts Robert can hear them. His wife warns his brother that Robert can hear his doubts. They pray around his bed. I can't see them behind the flimsy curtain, but I know they are bowing their heads.

Because I am "a regular," the nurses let my mom in early. She's already sitting in her chair underneath the TV when Tracy and I roll in.

We sit silently for awhile, and Tracy takes a blood sample by unclipping one of my IVs and letting blood run from the tube into a capsule. My mouth waters as the red blood snakes down. It reminds me of 7-Eleven ICEEs, of pulling the lever and watching the cherry descend into my cup. When Tracy does this, my mom stares at the wall and wrings her fingers like they are wet.

Trix visits today. She tries to climb into bed with me, but my mom pulls her back by her shoulders after she jostles me. She scoots a chair next to my bed and updates me on gossip. Her storytelling is so animated, and I fixate on her gestures, like I'm waiting for the end of a magic trick scarf. She drapes herself along the side of my bed, and I notice how pliable her body is, how it seems as if I could fold it into an accordion. I remember my body being like this, like it could stretch as if there were no limit.

Trix tells me that she's in charge of collecting my homework while I'm out sick. "There's a lot! But don't worry," she whispers, "I'm going to get you all the answers." She holds up a word-of-the day flip calendar from my English teacher, Ms. Storms, who knows how much I like words. I like that there are so many of them. "Today's word is 'knackered,'" Trix says, imitating a teacher's voice. She laughs. "Knackered!" Her face suddenly turns serious. "You must be really knackered," she says, then places the calendar on my stomach so I can look at it. Tracy walks in and suggests that Trix braid my hair the way her hair is braided: in alternating strips across the top of her head. She looks like the pioneer American Girl doll, and my mouth moistens at the thought of someone touching my head. My mom and Tracy help prop me up with pillows, and Trix asks Tracy about her favorite makeup brands as she weaves pieces of my greasy hair together.

Before she leaves, she tells me about all the disorders she's learning about in her AP psychology class. She's already read ahead to the sociology section, and her eyes widen to moons when she tells us about her reading.

"So in like the forties, or fifties, or something, there was this sociologist named Talcott Parsons. So, Parsons was basically this dude who believed in functionality—like everyone has a role in society, and they should stick to that role. So when a person gets sick, he basically argued that being sick was um, what's the word, *deviant*, like a form of *deviance*, like you chose to go against your role, or society, or whatever. So, there's also what he called like the 'physician's role' I think, and it's essentially the concept that society has created a role for a doctor to make sure you get better, and you, like, give up your regular rights to yourself and your body by being sick, and it's the doctor's role to, like, make you better, whatever that means, er, whatever it takes. So, like, basically the theory claims you have no rights."

Trix's eyes jump between me and my mom. "It's messed up!" she says. "How these dudes established theories, and like, how people just believed them to be true. *Alsooo* did you know there's a psychological disorder that compels you to eat your own flesh?"

Visiting hours end, and Trix floats away, giving Robert an embarrassed wave as she walks through the door. She seems to take all the air with her when she leaves. I am exhausted from my stillness and from all the listening.

"I'm so happy you girls have each other," my mom says, her palm distributing grease along my forehead. I think of the last time we were all together, at the Dairy Queen drive-thru, giggling in my mom's hand-me-down Honda. Trix was telling my mom about how mad our choir director Wally got when all the show choir girls braided their ponytail wigs together. We laughed between bites of cheesecake ice cream, then hissed when our brains began to freeze. Later that night, my mom agreed to let me spend Saturday evening—what should have been mother-daughter night—with Trix at the mall. We were actually planning to shotgun beers at Harmony Faulken's barn party, maybe flash the boys behind Harmony's dad's tractors. But plans changed. Instead, I was rushed to the closest city with an ER, not able to breathe, my left arm a dummy arm, hot and purple, a phantom lead foot pressing down on my chest.

Thursday

In the morning, Tracy brings me two drawings from the children's wing of the hospital: a sunset and a sunrise, but I cannot differentiate the two. She hangs them on the bare wall next to my bed. One drawing was made using crayons, the other with thick, bleeding markers. These are my new friends. We nap the morning away together.

I wake and feel my bladder. Before I call Tracy for the bedpan, I have a fleetingly sober moment. How the fuck did I get here? Inching my hand closer to the call button is a great effort, like my hand is trapped in a mirage. I accept the fact that I can't use my brain, but then I realize that I can't use my body, either. Or wait—*it was the other way around first*. I begin to laugh.

Tracy enters, her head cocked to the side. "You are always laughing, my sweet Ryann," she says, shaking her head. "Did I give you laughing gas by accident?"

Tracy gently lifts my pelvis and slides the bedpan underneath me. The bedpan is the color of beige from fifty years ago, or maybe the inside of an organ. While I pee I focus on the crescent of Tracy's nails, which are gently attached to me, making marks on me. When I'm finished and she pulls the pan out from under me, I pretend the marks she made are tattoos. Little moth wings.

Tracy leaves, and a band of student doctors file in for another lesson. The teaching physician, a broad-shouldered man with thick, curly blond hair and bristly eyelashes, smiles at me as he talks to his students about My Rare Condition. This performance is clockwork; I tune it out. Curly Hair moves so he's standing at the center of my bed. He raises my blanket and gown to expose my left thigh, also exposing my vagina. "Whoops!" he says and covers me back up.

"Usually with this condition, the stent is in the upper thigh. Apologies," he says to me and winks. He turns the students' attention to my left arm, which is elevated and sitting atop a flat surface, wrapped to the approximate size of Popeye's forearm. There are two lines running out of the gauze, leading to monitors that squawk loudly. I do mental gymnastics to try to understand how Dr. Curly Hair missed my arm—the loudest extremity in the room—and went straight for the thigh, but I'm too tired to understand mistakes. They discuss My Rare Condition with serious tones while their eyes slide onto every part of my body but my face. Then they are gone. I lie still and mentally tally how many strangers have seen my naked body in the last few days of my new life here. I think of my first pubic hair, and how I plucked it with my mom's tweezers. I plucked them all until I dared try her razor. After that, I was always smooth.

When Trix asked me if I would show her a few months later, I did. "I want to look like Julia," she told me, referring to one of the older ballerinas. Julia is completely shaven. We know this because all of the ballerinas change costumes in the same dank locker room during recitals. The year Trix and I dance to Judy Garland's "April Showers," we notice Julia's bare vagina as she changes into her final costume, a white one-piece tutu that has a complicated pattern of straps on the back. I remember she asked me to help her untwist two of the elastic straps before she went to dip her toes in rosin. After the recital that evening, I walked through the parking lot to my mom's car and saw Julia and her best friend Rebecca with a group of older boys. Julia was wearing a puffy coat over her costume, and their booming laughs echoed through the enclosed lot. The tulle from her skirt was tucked into the backside of her leotard, making her tutu into a rabbit tail poof. The boys took turns slapping her butt as she and Rebecca skittered and squealed.

I fall asleep and dream that I'm lying in a bed that is the size of a hotel pool, wedged between pillows that are actually my dogs. Dr. Bishop's back is turned, and he is discussing something with a large group of people. It's a stage of people. It's him surrounded by people on a stage. I say something, but no one turns to look at me. I say it again. I shout. I scream, and blood sprays onto my dogs. They lick their paws. I glance down and notice my tits and skin have been completely removed, and I'm bleeding out. Tracy appears, wearing a prom dress, her hair wet, and her face creased with layers of bronzer the wrong shade for her face. "Isn't it nice?" she says to me. "You can say anything you want! FUCK YOU!" she screams, and then gives me a wink. She pronounces her "K" like

Wally taught me—the movement begins in the diaphragm and ends in the back of the throat. My blood tastes like a pecan pie my mom once made. A dancer from the next county over named Beth is twirling on the corner of the stage, her spins so exact I never see her face.

When I emerge from this dream, I hear shuffling around Robert's bed. Nurses are calling his name loudly, bumping my pellucid curtain, their bodies like faces from a parallel universe. I understand what they are doing. Robert is awake. He is moaning. He has survived. And now they are telling him to hold tight, the doctor is coming.

Friday

My mom is late for visiting hours, but I only know because she announces "I'm late" when she arrives, flushed, pacing at the foot of my bed. Robert's family has already come and gone, as Robert was moved during visiting hours to another wing of the hospital, a wing for people in recovery. My mom apologizes for being late, says she's been on with the insurance company, then trails off. I tell her that it's okay, don't worry, I've been watching *Judge Judy.*

"Where's Robert?" she asks with a sharp intake of breath.

Tracy glides in and touches my mom's shoulder. "He woke from his coma," she says, smiling from ear to ear. "He's doing much better now."

Visiting hours are in the afternoon, I know, and I've been spending my morning having a power breakfast of morphine and tapioca. Judge Judy has been yelling at two women, Kelly and Kayla, for their violent behavior toward one another. I get why they're in trouble, but I'm on their side. Judge Judy is hammering them, just biting their heads off. In fact, from one camera angle, it looks like she could fit their heads into her gaping mouth. The former part of my breakfast has been making the edges a bit fuzzier than usual, and I don't notice, at first, that my mom is crying.

"He's gonna be okay," she whispers to Tracy, a single tear jumping ship.

Tracy takes both of my mom's shoulders now, the pink of her acrylics blinding me. She's speaking to my mom firmly, and her body seems to balloon above my mom, my mom's shoulders bowing inward, almost disappearing entirely. I notice, for the first time, how small my mom really is, her limbs like ribbons. Her elegant but tired fingers. The endless length of her neck. Tracy is saying something about "your daughter," something about how "she's in the best care for this." She says this as she leads my mom out into the hallway.

I realize they are talking about me. I think back to the moment in the ER when the doctor told us it was very bad. The nurses made a sign for my ER door, warning everyone of My Rare Condition. I was not allowed to walk, I was not allowed to be touched until Dr. Bishop arrived.

In the ER, I lay on the crusty paper bed and thought about Beth from Delaware County. We'd competed in dance competitions together since we were six. I thought about how earlier in the year she had collapsed while crossing the street. Our dance team sent her mom flowers. The newspaper said her best friend had been with her when it happened, had let out a wail that a local witness first thought was some kind of animal. We had competed against each other in a regional show the week before it happened. I beat her by two points, and she gave me a hug instead of a handshake when they announced the results.

I might die just like Beth died, except here in this room, with the peeling ceiling. I think about the ER, when the ER doctor told us about the blood clot the length of a pencil in my arm, and the blood clots in my lungs, and I think about how my mom told him, crying, that a girl we knew had just died from a blood clot, so how could this happen—to two girls—why did this happen to my daughter? And how he said, again, "It's very rare," and then slipped out of the room.

I want to talk to Beth. I want to ask her if she knows that she is dead. I want to tell her that no one talks about how she died, just that she is dead. I feel fury for her. I want to survive this for her, so I can look everyone in the face and tell them they are all cowards for not grieving her more, for not writing newspaper stories about the gruesome way a special girl could just die.

All of you, fucking cowards!!!

Beth had competed with "Cell Block Tango," a song choice I applauded due to its slower, more challenging count and due to the controversy it created among the dance moms. I played it safe with "You Make Me Feel So Young." I wore tiny shorts and a top hat, which I think pleased the judges, plus the way I curved my neck toward them during my barrel turn. I remember Beth's routine included pantomiming: Beth pulling the noose taut on her neck; Beth sashaying into a kitchen knife; Beth crumbling to the floor, mocking her boyfriend's death by arsenic. Her face was round and glassy like a compass, her spins a manifesto.

My thumb finds the red button just as my mom walks in, led by Tracy and a woman I have not yet met. My mom's face is flushed and glistening. They are Charlie's Angels. No. They are Charlie's Angels except they are just Angels. The woman I have not yet met is my surgical anesthesiologist. She pumps my fingers and says that she is here to tell me everything, except what I don't want to know.

I say something I don't remember, and they all laugh, so I find it's okay to laugh, too. Tracy pencils in my vitals, and tells me I'm looking good, sister. The thing is, I still haven't been able to look in a mirror, but I feel safe enough to fall asleep surrounded by these women. When I wake up in an hour, my mom will be talking to my grandma, who will spend the night with her at the Ronald McDonald House. They'll both wear socks to bed, and they'll whisper to each other until one of them falls asleep. When I wake up tomorrow, Tracy will be there to softly hoist my hips upward as I release into the flat bucket, and then she'll deliver me to the operating wing of the hospital, where Dr. Bishop will cut me open and cut out my rib to rid me of danger. *Pul-mo-nary em-bo-lism. Deep vein throm-bo-sis.* The syllables will anchor my tongue to my throat and my throat to my neck and my neck to my bed, my keeper. I won't remember how I got there. I won't feel the many hands on me, the scalpel, the saw, the tube in my throat. I won't know about deliverance, yet, not then, but later.

Saturday

I am sixteen and feel like shit. I have a new body, with a hole in it, and the nurse with the spiky hair needs me to stand so he can wheel me to imaging, where they're going to take a picture of their work. Dr. Bishop operated on me for four hours, and now I'm in a recovery room with a framed imitation of *Starry Night* hanging at the foot of my bed. My sunset is gone. My sunrise is gone. My morphine is gone. I don't remember saying goodbye to Tracy. No one asked me if I wanted to be here.

Spiky Hair guides me by my elbow into a sunken wheelchair, where I'm certain I'll be swallowed and disappear. We whiz down a hallway, and I'm dizzied by the passing scenery: a series of Pop Art prints, the anxious Lichtensteins beaming; a toddler escaping from her mother; a section of our journey framed by lime green walls, the most offensive color I've ever seen. I guess I'm mumbling because Spiky Hair reassures me that we're almost there. Then he puts on my brake and leaves me sitting in a hallway.

I have a memory of being wheeled to the operating room. It was just like in the movies, passing ceiling tiles and the under-chins of strangers. The doctors carry on conversations around me, through me, never to me. I wonder where I am, if I am even here. I slipped under so quickly I didn't realize it was happening. Now I am here. From there to here.

Spiky Hair returns to wheel me into the imaging room, where they take a picture of the lung that had been invaded with blood clots, the ones that scared the ER doctor, the ones that drained all the color from my mom's face. He scoots me back to my *Starry* bed, and after that I sleep for a very long time, dreaming of nothing, or maybe of absence.

Later, a physical therapist shows me exercises to get my arm back to normal. "You'll bounce back," he says with an airy grin. A nurse with plastic fingers appears to remove my catheter, which was inserted during surgery. She tugs and it's over but I remember, fleetingly, when Tracy and the other nurses changed my sheets in the ICU, and how I imagined my body then as woolly, cotton candy. A doctor glides in to report that my X-ray came back just as they wanted it: no more first rib obstructing blood from entering the subclavian vein in my arm. *It's gone!* We learn that tendons and tissues and miscellaneous body things will grow into the space where my rib used to be. Also the clots in my lungs, he says, will eventually disintegrate, over time. *Oh.* He's ecstatic, dismissive, and I've stopped wondering where Dr. Bishop is. "You can finally get outta here!" He dazzles with his smile and then he is gone. My mom brings me a burger to celebrate, and its tinny, distant taste is too much for me. I force a croak, which is meant to be a laugh. "Is there any pudding?" My friends visit, and their chatter is disorienting. The recital was a bust, they tell me. I guess my crown popped off Stephanie's head halfway through the second movement and Tessa slipped on it and bruised her tailbone. "Karma!" Trix shouts, but I'm not sure what karma means anymore. They leave and I don't miss them. I float through the rest of the day in stillness and in quiet.

Then it is tomorrow, and my mom is pulling the car up to the curb, and I am wearing pants, and a bra to silence my tits, to contain me. Out of my hospital gown, I feel in disguise. I think to myself, *So this is what it's like to have a body.* I finally know, or I know too soon. People rush past me. Doctors look beyond me. I pass a mirror in the lobby of the hospital, and I touch my face to make sure she does the same. I look her in the eyes and promise to keep our secret.

Joanna Demkiewicz's writing has appeared in *Midwest Review*, *Literary Hub*, *Guernica*, *Nylon*, and *The Los Angeles Review*. She cofounded *The Riveter* and produced a limited-edition magazine called *Before I Became Time* to raise money for the Minnesota Prison Writing Workshop. She lives in Minneapolis.

Editor's Note

Like all the best speculative fiction, Jason Fernandes's "Love-sick" does more than create a plot out of a premise. While the premise is fascinating—a pill taken with a partner that guarantees continuous, long-lasting love and attraction—the heart of the story prods at the very nature of our shared humanity. It explores universal questions: What does it mean to love someone? Is love made deeper and stronger when it's challenged by the messy stuff of life—our compromises, our insecurities, our sacrifices and fears? Does such a love have more value than one that skips the roller coaster of long-term relationships, the drama mixed with monotony, and instead glides along on the gooey feelings of new attraction? "Lovesick" doesn't offer easy answers, but with sharp, witty writing, expertly developed characters, and quick, restrained storytelling, we are, as we always must be, left with our own questions.

Adrianne Finlay, Assistant Editor
North American Review

Lovesick

Jason Fernandes

THAT THERE WAS A MEDICAL TERM FOR WHAT HAPPENED to me did, in fact, give me some relief. That the term involved the word *crisis* only vindicated my fear, made my reaction seem almost nonchalant in retrospect. An oculogyric *crisis*. The word was usually reserved for problems that were global or existential in their scope, the stuff of nightmares and great art, things like *financial crisis* and *midlife crisis* and *Cuban Missile Crisis*. And here was my crisis, at home in this club of catastrophes: a crisis where you lose control of your eyes and they roll into the back of your head, literally *roll*, like beach balls spinning helplessly in a pool, and of course I should have realized at the time that it was a sign of things to come.

It happened during one of our Sunday dinners. Frances had started this tradition where, every Sunday, we cooked a random meal, split a bottle of wine, and generally tried to act as childlike as possible to prepare ourselves for the drudgery of the workweek. This week, we'd made burritos full of marshmallows and orange slices; they were delightfully disgusting.

Frances was sitting across from me with Harold, our Boston terrier, in her lap. One second everything was normal, Frances laughing as she tried biting an orange slice hard enough to make it squirt on me, her eyes watery from citrus or laughter. But then she was sliding out of frame, until I could see only the top of her head beneath an expanse of scratched drywall and ceiling.

Even then, during the onset of this crisis, simply having Frances somewhere in my field of vision was enough to fill me with warmth. It didn't occur to me to wonder how much of this feeling was generated by Orexis.

I closed my eyes. I hoped Frances didn't think I'd rolled my eyes at her. I opened them again, and for a second, I thought I'd imagined it; there was Frances, light of my life, giggling as she let Harold lick her chin. But then she was gone, my eyes once again exerting their newfound agency.

"Frances," I said. I tried to look at her, but she kept sliding away.

"What the hell," said Frances.

"Help," I managed. Everything was sliding away; it was like I was doing backflips without leaving my chair. Every time I opened my eyes, there'd be a split second when they looked straight ahead, a false promise of stability, but then they'd start their nauseating roll upward, pitching my world into chaos.

"Oh god, oh *god*," Frances was saying. She'd taken my head in her hands, a gesture both loving and diagnostic, but now I could hear her pacing the living room, perhaps traumatized by what she'd seen. Somewhere nearby, I could hear Harold scurrying and wheezing, mimicking her panicked movements.

I became aware that my neck was twisted upward and to the left. Moving it felt nearly impossible; my neck, apparently, was also no longer mine to control. I experienced a brief moment of depersonalization, observing myself with a crooked neck and eyes rolled into the back of my skull. I wondered if this would slowly spread to my entire body, as some ancient and aggrieved spirit had its way with me.

"Okay, thank you, okay," I heard Frances say.

Within twenty minutes we were in the emergency room. Frances kissed the top of my head and told me to wait while she spoke with someone. She was fierce when she needed to be, and hypercompetent, and the part of me that wasn't panicking about losing control of my body was feeling grateful for her protection.

I sat in a squishy chair in the waiting room that I imagined had held thousands of dying bodies before me. The room reeked of disinfectant. More than once, I had the unpleasant experience of opening my eyes and having them roll upward until I was staring directly into a fluorescent ceiling light.

Frances was struggling to explain my condition to a triage nurse. "Just *look* at him," I heard her say.

There were others in the waiting room, some of whom were groaning in pain. I felt competitive with them. I had to demonstrate that my needs were more immediate than theirs. I angled my body toward the intake counter and tried to lock eyes with the triage nurses, but they kept slipping out of frame. I let out a low moan and lolled out my tongue for good measure.

Some combination of Frances's advocacy and my horrid appearance did seem to accelerate the process. I'd only just begun to go through my mental Rolodex of happy memories with Frances, searching for an image to hold onto as I drew my last breath, when we were ushered into an examination room.

As soon as the curtains were drawn, Frances threw her arms around me.

"It's going to be okay," she said.

"I think I'm being possessed by a demon," I said. I could feel the beginnings of a migraine, as though someone were slowly inserting a steel rod into my brain. I decided to keep my eyes closed unless strictly necessary; the rolling had started making me queasy.

I felt Frances move her face in front of mine. I knew its every line and curve. What if I had to live without seeing it again?

"Knock, kno-ock," said a lilting voice behind the curtain. A pause, then the tinny scrape of the curtains being forced open. I felt Frances move away.

"Mr. Robles, tell me what's going on," the voice said.

"His eyes keep rolling, and his neck is tilted. Look," said Frances. "It's like he's lost control of his muscles."

"I'm being possessed by a demon," I said.

"How long has he been like this?" The doctor directed this question to Frances.

"About an hour. We were just eating dinner and then suddenly this happened."

"Has this ever—"

"Never happened before, no," said Frances.

"First time for everything," I added. I braved a look at the doctor. In the second before my eyes migrated north, I locked eyes with a short, bald man with a pubic goatee. I was reminded of a cartoon turtle. He quickly slid out of view.

I heard the scribbling of pen on clipboard. "Are you taking any medications?"

"No," I said.

"Just Orexis," Frances corrected. "We're both on it."

"Ah," said the doctor. More scribbling. "Which lines?"

"Blue and yellow."

"My head is going to explode."

Scribble scribble. Then what sounded like a page being folded in half. "Oculogyric crisis is a known side effect of adamafil," the doctor said. "Atroxafil, too."

"You've seen this before?" asked Frances.

The doctor breathed loudly. "It's in the literature. It's a rare side effect, but definitely associated with Orexis."

It took me a minute to digest what he was saying. He couldn't possibly mean, he couldn't be saying—

"I would recommend that you stop taking Orexis immediately, Mr. Robles," he said.

Silence erupted between us as we considered the doctor's words. How could he suggest such a thing? It felt like a gross breach of etiquette, like he'd propositioned Frances and was waiting to see how both of us reacted.

"But," said Frances. "But everyone takes it."

Another crushing silence, broken a few interminable moments later by the sticky salivary sound of the doctor opening his mouth to speak. "I know this isn't easy to hear," he said.

Through my blindness, I imagined the doctor staring at his clipboard, either feeling or affecting an appropriate level of awkwardness.

"How about you, doc?" I managed. "You on the blues? The full marital suite?"

"That's neither here nor there," he said. But of course he was.

"We've been taking it for four years," Frances said. "Why would this just happen now?"

I tried to imagine our relationship from the doctor's perspective, stripped down to its clinically significant facts penned in shorthand on an intake form: *30 y/o M-F couple / cohabitating / together 5 years / started Orexis after year 1.* The objective truth was that our relationship was about as pedestrian as it got, from the Judeo-Christian choreography of our lovemaking to our decision to foster, then adopt, our beloved arthritic terrier. But somehow I wanted to convey to the doctor how special we were, how extraordinary our love was in its ordinariness, if only to make him feel the gravity of his suggestion that I stop taking the pills that bound us.

"If you're interested, there's a new version of the drug in clinical trials. It's intravenous, administered biweekly. Early results seem promising."

"We'd have to get injections?" Frances asked.

"You can read up on it here." The doctor handed something to Frances, and I guessed—correctly, I'd later learn—that it was a glossy brochure featuring photos of smiling couples.

Pen on clipboard again, then a quick tearing of paper. "Your symptoms should resolve in a few hours. In the meantime, I'll give you something for the pain."

The doctor pushed open the curtain partition. "Many couples find they can manage just fine without the meds."

OVER THE NEXT few days, Frances and I became newly awkward around each other. We tiptoed around the subject, but we were both clearly waiting to see whether I'd fall out of love with her now that I no longer had the pills to help.

We'd been on the standard regimen: blue pills to stay in love with each other, yellow pills to ensure that we didn't fall in love with anyone else. Part of what made the waiting so excruciating was that we didn't know how much we relied on the pills. It would have been easier if we knew that there was no love between us absent the blues, that the only thing keeping us from running off with other people was the yellows. But that wasn't how it worked. Most couples started taking Orexis after just one year, before the end of the honeymoon phase, precisely because doing so allowed them to maintain the fiction that they didn't actually need them, that they were merely taking them as a prophylactic measure and to smooth out any awkward imbalances in attraction.

If there was an imbalance in attraction between us, I think both of us would have assumed that Frances was the one who needed the pills more.

On our first date, Frances had seemed less entertained by me than by her power over me.

"This is the part where you hold my hand," she'd said as we walked from dinner to a cocktail bar, interlacing her fingers with my own.

When I walked her back to her car, she stopped and grabbed my jacket, pulling my face inches from hers. "This is the most important moment," she said. "Don't mess it up."

Frances always seemed to play two roles, oscillating between an ironic observer of herself, as though intimacy were a joke she wanted to make it clear she was in on, and a vulnerable person who wanted nothing more than to be loved unconditionally. When she suggested, at the end of our first year, that we take the aphrodisiac of the masses, I believed it to be the most romantic gesture Frances could offer. To suggest that we take the most traditional step for couples in our position, to commit our bodies and brains to love one another exclusively, to be common schmucks in a monogamous arrangement: She might as well have proposed then and there.

And it worked. For the next four years, our relationship was nearly perfect. It didn't matter to us whether or how much we were relying on Orexis; we were in love, and happy, and that was all that mattered.

But now, it was all in jeopardy. Our apartment had started to feel less like a home and more like a museum of our relationship, full of artifacts that reminded me of how hopelessly intertwined our lives were, how many decisions we'd made under the assumption that we'd stay together indefinitely. Here was all the furniture we'd picked out together; there was the pile of unopened mail addressed to both of us, with account statements reflecting our shared assets and liabilities; and there was Harold, our little tachycardiac munchkin, who'd probably die of a panic attack if he knew that his co-parents might split up. How could I live without Frances? Who even was I without Frances?

THE FIRST DIFFERENCE I noticed, three days after the ER visit, was that my world was suddenly teeming with beautiful people. They were everywhere: smiling at me from bus decals advertising Orexis, stepping on my foot in the crush of bodies boarding the metro, frowning at me during my mid-year performance review. I felt like I was fifteen again, at the mercy of my hormones. In a training I led at work, I couldn't stop looking at one of the new hires and his chiseled jawline. Then I'd catch myself staring, and I'd make a point to look at every other participant before letting my eyes wander back to him again, some distant and unprofessional part of me imagining myself tracing my fingers along his cheekbones, his lips. Later, in the cafeteria, I was so distracted by the athletic figure of a woman in the marketing department that I overheated my leftover lasagna, creating a crime scene in the microwave that took most of my lunch break to clean.

But I still felt the same way toward Frances. When I got back to my desk after lunch, I found a package waiting for me: flowers, an assortment of fruit, and a card. The front of the card featured a drawing of a goateed turtle in a lab coat, with a speech bubble that said, "*Frances loves you*, Mr. Robles." When I opened the card, I had to stifle my laughter; the inside featured a detailed drawing of the turtle receiving fellatio from another turtle.

I propped the card on my desk—folded so only the front was visible—so I could look at the words *Frances loves you* throughout the day.

It wasn't until later that evening, when we ran into Frances's college friends at the grocery store, that the changes began to feel significant.

As usual, the store was packed with couples. I'd read that over 90 percent of couples were on Orexis, so I'd been playing a silent game as we shopped, trying to figure out which couples were on the pills just by looking. I thought I saw it in the placid smiles, the strides in rhythm—those couples whose movements looked synchronized, like they were different appendages of the same organism.

Then one of the couples—whose movements were decidedly *not* in sync—mistook my concentrated stare for an attempt at recognition.

"Is that . . . Eric?" said the taller of the two, who I then recognized as Russell. He was accompanied by his partner, Carter. "And Frances?"

Frances screeched and greeted them with a joint hug, which caused Russell and Carter to bump heads.

I'd met them a few times before. I'd never liked Carter much, but I'd always enjoyed spending time with Russell. At their most recent college reunion, while Frances and Carter made the rounds with their former classmates, Russell made a point to hang back and spend time with me. He kept joking that he hated those kinds of events, but given the number of people whose faces lit up when they saw him, I had the sense that he was just saying that to make me feel better about keeping him from his friends.

This time, though, I immediately knew something was different. I guess I'd always thought of Russell as beautiful in an abstract sense, but I'd forgotten what it was like to *feel* that attraction, the kick in the midsection that leaves you short of breath and fumbling for words. But there I was, clutching a bag of frozen green beans, worried that Russell would be able to feel my heart pounding when my chest touched his as we hugged hello. He smelled like vanilla and leather. Could he tell I was smelling him?

"Eric had this crazy reaction to the O," Frances was saying. "We had to go to the ER."

Carter and Russell exchanged a look. I stared at the floor.

"Did you have the eye thing?" Russell asked. He made a face intended to represent an oculogyric crisis. It looked like someone on the receiving end of intense pleasure.

I tried, uselessly, to prevent my cheeks from flushing. "Yeah. How did—"

"You're still doing it," he said.

I grabbed my face, horrified. Russell and Frances laughed.

I rolled my eyes and flipped Russell off, hoping the gesture would come across as playful. He grinned at me, and I was reborn. I was gripping the bag of green beans so tight it might burst.

Before we parted ways, Russell suggested we all get dinner this week. His eyes lingered on mine as he said this. He said he and Carter didn't take Orexis—if I weren't melting under Russell's gaze, I would've felt proud for guessing this correctly— and they'd be happy to share with us their experience of love au naturel.

Frances was thrilled at the idea. She was less thrilled, however, when I suggested they come over on Sunday.

After Russell and Carter left, Frances turned on me. "What about our date night?"

Date night. Sunday night dinners. Of course—how could I have forgotten? "I wasn't really thinking about that," I admitted. "I guess I forgot."

"You forgot," Frances repeated.

"We can just do date night on Saturday?"

Frances shrugged and pushed the cart farther down the aisle. *If you don't care, neither do I*, her shrug seemed to say.

As Frances continued on, I lingered in the ice cream section, appreciating my cornucopia of choices. So many brands and flavors competing for my attention. I held the door open long enough that it became opaque with fog.

It took me a few minutes to find Frances—she was already halfway through checking out. I caught up with her and scanned my pint.

Frances stopped my hand with hers. "What's that?"

I looked down at the ice cream. "Ice cream?"

"You're lactose intolerant."

"Only a little," I said, placing the ice cream in a bag. "I just saw it and was kind of craving it. I haven't had it in a while."

Frances's eyes bounced from me to the ice cream and then back to me. "Ice cream," she said.

FRANCES USUALLY STAYED up later than me and slept in later than me, but when I woke up the next morning, she was sitting upright, already awake. She was staring straight ahead, her face blank, but her red and puffy eyes told me she'd been crying. I felt certain she'd been awake for hours—possibly all night.

"Hey," I whispered. "What's wrong?"

Her voice was dry and scratchy when she finally spoke. "I'm going to stop taking it, too." She kept staring at the opposite wall, as though afraid to look at me as she said this.

This had never occurred to me. Of course it made sense for her to stop. It was unfair to ask her to keep taking it once I was no longer on it. But still, could we survive both of us stopping Orexis?

I nuzzled my head into her neck. "We'll get through this," I said.

SUNDAY FINALLY ARRIVED and brought with it Russell, holding a bottle of red wine and grinning at us from our landing. He wore a tight V-neck romper that teased his smooth, muscular chest, and how could I not imagine what he looked like without it?

Frances, Russell, and Carter spent most of the dinner reminiscing about their college years. I kept myself busy by moving plates in and out of the kitchen. When I ran out of tasks, I mostly scratched Harold and drank my wine. When I found myself staring too long at Russell, I made sure to give Frances and Carter an equal amount of eye contact.

I thought I'd done a pretty good job of being nonchalant about this crush, but when we all began to migrate from the dining room to the living room, Frances pulled me into the side hallway.

"You like Russell," she said.

Her gaze was a challenge that I instantly backed away from. I could feel my cheeks burning. I craned my neck to see if our guests could see or hear us.

Frances laughed. "It's okay," she said. "You know they're in an open relationship, right?"

I stood there stupidly, agape.

She added, "You should go for it," before walking into the bathroom and shutting the door.

I stayed in the hallway for as long as I could before I felt it would become obvious that something had transpired between us. I had no idea what to make of it—was she teasing me? Testing me? We'd never discussed being open before. I decided to just ignore it for the moment.

While Frances was in the bathroom, I refilled everyone's wine-glasses—including my own, twice. There was a space on the couch next to Russell, but this felt like a trap, so I perched on an ottoman in the middle of the living room. Harold immediately jumped into my lap.

"So," Russell said. He swirled his glass, an innocuous gesture that I somehow felt was imbued with sexual significance. "What's it like being off the O?"

I could feel the heat of Russell's gaze. I imagined I must have been blushing so much it would look like I was having an allergic reaction.

"No, no, no," called Frances, who had reemerged from the

bathroom. "We invited you so *you* could tell *us* how to cope without O."

She plopped down on the floor beside me. "So, tell us. Do you fight a lot? Do you have less sex?"

Carter rolled his eyes and turned to us. "When I look at Russ, I don't just see a beautiful face that makes me feel gooey inside."

"That's what I see when I look at Russ," said Frances.

Me too, I thought.

"I see all our fights. I see our sacrifices." He reached out and held Russell's hand. "I see the work we put in to make our relationship stronger. I see all of it."

"And he still feels gooey inside," Russell added.

Harold pawed at my leg, a reminder to keep petting him. It occurred to me that Harold would never need a pill to love me unconditionally, nor I to keep loving him.

"I don't know," I said. As soon as I started speaking, I felt the clumsy weight of my own tongue. I wasn't sober enough to articulate myself properly, but no longer sober enough to care. "It sounds like you're describing the sunk-cost fallacy. Or Stockholm syndrome. Or some project at work that's been giving you so much hell you've finally convinced yourself it's important." Frances gave me a warning look, but I avoided her eyes as I continued. "What if all the bad stuff isn't indicative of some deeper love? What if it's just bad stuff, and it's better not to have it?"

Carter snorted. "Or what if, when your limbic system is drowning in adamafil, the problems are still there, but you just don't see them until they're too big for you to deal with?"

"How would you know if you haven't taken it?" I instantly regretted my tone—I sounded like a child in a spat with a sibling.

"We have."

Three heads rounded on Russell. Four, if you count Harold, who seemed drawn to Russell's soft baritone.

"You total fraud," said Frances, giving him a playful kick.

Russell smiled, and the room suddenly felt brighter. "We're not still on it. This was years ago."

Something in Russell's tone told us a story was coming, so we let his words resonate while we settled in for the tale. I was grateful for the story as an excuse to look at Russell for an extended period of time. It was ludicrous how enjoyable it was to simply look at his face, to drink it in.

But the longer I looked, the more I began to feel a creeping unease. Before Frances confronted me, this had just been a silly crush. But now it was as though she'd spoken it into existence, and it was a thing that had to be dealt with.

I tried to focus on the content of Russell's story instead of its source. He and Carter had been in a triad with someone named Phil, apparently, and all three of them had been taking the blues. This revelation wasn't too surprising: Orexis had led to a rise in polyamorous relationships because the pills allowed people to share love more equitably among all partners. Russell and Carter were happy in their triad for several months, but at some point, things started to deteriorate. Carter and Phil started fighting more. Phil accused Carter of trying to steal Russell. Carter, meanwhile, was apparently trying to steal Russell, and he started trying to convince Russell to end things with Phil.

They all discovered later that they'd mixed up their bottles of Orexis, and the formula didn't work on the person it wasn't made for. Without the blues, Carter and Phil could barely stand one another.

"But Russ and I discovered that we still loved each other," Carter was saying. "So here we are."

Turning my attention back to Carter, I had a small realization about the mechanics of Orexis. Though I'd never liked Carter—I never understood what Russell saw in him—it occurred to me now that this dislike had likely always been fueled by my attraction to Russell. While the Orexis had been blocking me from feeling the attraction to Russell, the attraction was still there beneath the surface, generating a dislike of his partner that I understood now to be nothing more than simple jealousy.

I looked over at Frances. Something in her expression made me certain she'd been watching me for quite a while. I tried sipping the dregs at the bottom of my glass, but I'd emptied it long ago.

I SPENT MOST of the next week browsing Orexis forums, searching for reasons I should be happy to be off the O. I read plenty of accounts from folks like me who were told to stop taking Orexis because of the side effects. Several people reported disregarding their doctor's orders, usually with gruesome results; some swore that over-the-counter alternatives worked just as well, without the side effects. The only posts I saw about the newer, injectable version were from people who were hoping to be admitted to the clinical trials.

I was particularly interested in the accounts of O-intolerant folks whose relationships survived without the drug. They were few and far between, to be sure, but the people who went cold turkey typically shared their experiences with religious fervor. They assured us lurkers: It wasn't just possible to have a happy relationship without Orexis; indeed, that was the *only* way to have a truly happy relationship. I suspected that at least one of these posts was written by Carter.

But if I'm being honest, it wasn't this online escapism that buoyed me through an otherwise dreadful week. It was the idea of seeing Russell again.

I probably should have questioned whether there was some connection between my fear of Frances leaving me and my eagerness to dive headfirst into a crush on some guy I barely knew. But off I went, daydreaming about futures where Russell and I eloped to Alaska and he spent his days shirtlessly chopping wood for our fireplace. Sometimes Frances was in these daydreams, too, and the three of us had formed a happy, stable triad, where we all loved one another without pharmaceutical help.

In the meantime, Frances and I continued to avoid each other. Some part of me knew that we should have been talking about this, perhaps fighting, having some honest discussions about what it meant for us to stop taking Orexis. But we'd never needed to work out our problems before. We lacked the vocabulary to do so.

On one particularly dreary evening in which Frances and I sat in silence on opposite sides of our living room, both texting other people, Frances suggested we break this bleak cycle and go out. I couldn't think of a reason not to, so an hour later we were outside of a club, passing a flask back and forth, shivering in line behind a dozen twentysomethings who were already too drunk to communicate without shouting. They wore trendy outfits that seemed designed to distinguish their generation from ours; in my jeans and button-down shirt, I felt like a chaperone on a school trip. Frances, on the other hand, could've fit right in: She'd gone for a somewhat gothic aesthetic that suited our mood and made her look classically cool.

Even after we made it inside, we stayed in line: The line to get in had become a line for drinks; the unflattering yellow streetlights were swapped for unflattering strobing black lights. A syncopated reggaeton beat was blasting; most of the people around us were swaying to it. Frances was dancing, too—it started as just a bobbing of her head, then she deftly spread the undulation throughout her body.

"Loosen up those legs, Señor Robles," she said, placing her hands on my hips.

I had a prudish urge to resist dancing anywhere other than the designated dance floor. I knew I was being the wettest of blankets, but I stayed rooted, feet glued in place.

"*Touch me, baby . . .*" Frances sang along with the chorus. She was smiling at me, trying to get me in the mood.

I could sense a decision point approaching. I could reciprocate her effort, try to enjoy the night, dance with her and hope our performance of happiness precipitated the real thing. Or I could continue to sulk.

"I don't know this song," I said.

"Yes, you do. Everyone knows this."

"Everyone but me, I guess."

Frances pulled away from me. "Why do you always do this? This whole no-one-understands-me thing?"

"I'm just saying I don't know the song."

"Cool. I'm going to go dance. Come find me when there's a song you know. Or don't."

She was halfway to the dance floor before I could protest. Her black clothes blended with the darkness of the club, absorbed it. I watched her head jostle through a thicket of bodies until I could no longer distinguish it as hers.

I ordered a whiskey sour at the bar before heading to the dance floor. Some sort of synth-heavy pop song was now blaring; I felt like I was in an MRI machine. When I found Frances, she was dancing with another guy, some beefy, tight-shirted college kid whose arms were the size of my legs. Her choice of dance partner seemed deliberate, designed to inflame the toxically masculine part of me. He was grinding on Frances from behind, and his hands were roving each of her legs, getting closer and closer to meeting in the middle.

It occurred to me that one of the things I'd lost since being off Orexis was a generous lens through which to view Frances's actions. Maybe love just meant always assuming the best intentions from your partner; maybe Orexis was more about empathy than attraction. Frances and I could choose to view each other's actions—my flirtation with Russell, her increasingly sexual dancing with this brute—as deriving from an insecurity about our own relationship and our sloppy attempts to communicate this insecurity to one another. Maybe, on Orexis, I'd look at Frances and feel what she was feeling, and my desire to make her happy would triumph over my own jealousy and hurt. Maybe someday there'll be a universal version of Orexis where you view everyone through this lens, not just your partner, where you see all these sweaty and striving people as beautiful and equally deserving of love, even the ones flailing like beached carp on the dance floor, even the ones feeling up your girlfriend a few feet in front of you.

But I felt none of that now. I retreated to the bar and ordered another drink. When I checked my phone, I saw that Russell had texted. Seeing his name on my phone's lock screen gave me a perverse, possessive sort of pleasure. I waited a moment before opening his message, savoring the feeling.

How's date night?

I responded immediately: *looking pretty grim. what're you up to?*

I'm at the Dolphin. Want to join?

I had no time to formulate a response; Frances sat down on a barstool to my right, leaving an empty seat between us. Sweat had caused some of her mascara to run, heightening her gothic aesthetic.

"How's Russell?" she asked.

I didn't want to give her the satisfaction of a reaction. "How's Tarzan? Teach him any words yet?"

Frances was smiling, but it wasn't in response to anything I'd said or done. "You know, I'd forgotten what it felt like to date you before Orexis."

Her eyes were crawling over me, and I felt like she was mentally cataloging all the flaws that she could finally see clearly without the rose-colored glasses of Orexis: my psoriatic, acne-scarred skin; my prematurely receding hairline; my birdlike, crooked nose with one nostril more prominent than the other. For the first time in four years, I felt self-conscious in front of her.

"Don't you feel it, too?" she asked. "Don't you feel the difference?"

"No," I lied. I drained the rest of my drink. "I love you. Do you still love me?"

"Sweetie," she said. She was smiling that inward smile again. "It's easy to love you. But it's hard to be attracted to you."

I tried to come up with some response, something that could

put back the broken pieces of this conversation. But all I felt now was hurt, felt it in my entire body, a child-being-bullied sort of hurt.

"What are you doing?" I managed.

The scene around me had become blurry—I had to blink away tears to see clearly. I became dimly aware that a bartender was watching this interaction unfold, and for some reason, it was important to me to hold myself together in front of him.

A new song started playing, and it appeared to exert a gravitational pull on Frances. She was swaying again, inching closer to the dance floor, this time making no attempt to get me to join her.

Before she disappeared into the crowd, she said, "I'm going to have fun tonight. You should, too."

After Frances disappeared, I ordered another drink and tried to ignore the void that was opening inside me.

The Dolphin was just a few blocks away. It was just Russell there tonight, apparently; Carter was out with his work friends. That was what Frances meant by having fun tonight, right?

My legs were carrying me before my mind caught up to them. Or maybe my mind never did catch up to them—it was still at the bar with Frances, and I was happy to leave it behind.

I don't remember what I said to Russell before I kissed him. Maybe we didn't talk at all. I just remember our mouths lapping against one another, occasionally clinking teeth, before he gently pushed me away and said, "You're drunk."

Russell sat with me at the bar while I drank water and tried to keep the void from swallowing me whole. I wanted to tell him that this was not the glorious union that I'd been envisioning in my head all week.

The reality of my situation was setting in, and it felt like it was closing in on me from all sides. My entire life was bound up with Frances: my finances, my friends, my memories from the past five years. Who would take Harold? How could we disentangle our lives? Wouldn't it be easier to just stay together, even if the pills no longer worked?

"Can I tell you a secret?" Russell said. He was looking at me with kindness, but I imagined it was the sort of kindness you'd direct at a child.

"I'm still taking O," he said. "The blue pills."

Half-formed thoughts sloshed around my mind. *Are you saying you don't love Carter*, I wanted to ask. *Why not leave him? Why not take the pills with someone else?* But in my fragile state, I trusted myself with only one-word responses. "What?"

"I pay for the prescription in cash so Carter doesn't see it on my credit card statement."

"Why?"

Russell smiled, and he looked at me as though the answer were too obvious to be said. "Let's get you home."

IT WASN'T HAROLD'S growls that woke me up the next morning, or the late-morning sun crashing through our living room windows. It was pain. Pain everywhere, the hangover duo of headache and nausea, topped off with a feeling of dread that had settled into my muscles like lead. I had to strain to recall what happened the night before, but whatever it was, the feeling in my body convinced me that it was dire, possibly irreversible.

I'd also ended up on the couch. I imagined that Frances was asleep in our bedroom, but I was afraid to look.

When I rolled over to pet my apologies to Harold, something crunched under my arm—the brochure the doctor had given us. Had I been reading it last night? The couple on the front beamed at me with those lobotomized smiles, promising me a return to the days of easy love on Orexis.

I flipped the brochure over. Emblazoned across the back was the phone number to enroll in the clinical trial. Beneath that was a fine-print list of warnings and possible side effects; this version of the drug had fewer known side effects, and, thankfully, none of them featured the word *crisis*.

At that moment, Frances emerged from the bedroom. She had one sock on and was wearing one of my old workout shirts, and her hair was a tangled mess. As she walked closer to me, I could see that tears had left streaks of eyeliner and mascara on her face. Her lower lip was trembling.

"I stained the pillows," she said, with a half laugh, half sob.

I handed Frances the brochure. I could feel her warmth, could feel my body instinctively wanting to be closer to hers. She opened her arms, and I folded into them.

Jason Fernandes is a lawyer and speculative fiction writer. He's a recipient of the Kurt Vonnegut Speculative Fiction Prize and a graduate of the Odyssey Writing Workshop. His fiction has appeared in *Weird Horror, Hemingway Shorts,* and the *North American Review*.

Editor's Note

What stands out in "The Faraday Cage" is its astonishing control—the quiet pressure it exerts from the opening paragraph never lets up, even as its emotional landscape expands. Lara Hughes writes with empathy and precision, crafting a story that resists easy moral binaries while guiding us into the fragile, intimate circuitry of grief, motherhood, and the deep static of loss. The piece moves with the slow, deliberate power of a ship turning at sea, revealing the layered tensions between memory, technology, and the unspeakable. I was particularly drawn to how Hughes captures the quiet surveillance of everyday life—the ways mothers watch sons, neighbors watch newcomers, and a telescope listens for stars. It's a story that hums long after it ends.

"The Faraday Cage" was selected as the winner of *The Arkansas International* 2023 Emerging Writer's Prize by judge Karen Thompson Walker, who praised the story's "subtle, unexpected tenderness" and the way it captures "a highly unusual setting where outcasts of various kinds find an unlikely sense of community." We were thrilled to publish it in *The Arkansas International* and even more thrilled to see it honored by the PEN/Dau Prize.

Sam Campbell, Managing Editor (2022–2024)
The Arkansas International

The Faraday Cage

Lara Hughes

THAT DAY, RILEY SAT IN THE PRINCIPAL'S OFFICE WITH her son, Noah, and decided on the move as the principal thrust out Noah's cell phone, almost ramming it into her face. She decided to accept her brother's offer. On-screen, a girl knelt. She pushed her lips out in a pouty kiss and angled her naked legs open. Noah's reply sat in a small green bubble under the picture: *u r beautiful.*

The girl, a senior at another high school, had, unprompted, sent this self-portrait to a handful of Dematha's freshman boys. But here in the office with its timeless air of pencil shavings, it was only Noah rebuked for explicit material. One of his friends had shared the photo in a group text, responses batted back and forth, and now that pack of boys faced expulsion with only a month left in the school year. Zero tolerance. The girl, the principal said, would meet with a counselor every week. Noah sat with his head in his hands. Tufts of dark hair stuck up through his fingers.

If his father were here, called to appear in the office *at once* as if he himself had broken the rule, Dean would tell the principal: bullshit. Easy way out, he'd say, the school not dealing with the real problem. He'd sit in that office until Noah returned to physics. "All the time in the world, Mr. Principal."

Riley stood and tried, like Dean would've, to coax this waxy bureaucrat into reason, to admonish him for unfairness. She could hear Dean's chummy protest. "What was she expecting? Offered herself right up." Hear the scrape of the razor against his lifted chin the next morning, after he'd settled the matter. "Sad, really, her needing all that."

But as Riley tried to channel Dean's convincing words, the principal slid Noah's phone across the desk. He folded his thick arms and widened his stance into an impenetrable wall. Her protests failed, met only with silence. The bell rang. It screamed through her. Quick feet and laughter flooded the hallways as if a spigot had burst.

"Pretty shitty, kicking a kid at rock bottom." She snatched Noah's phone. Dean often said she backed down one moment too soon.

"Again, we're so sorry about your husband's passing." The principal shrugged. "But rules are rules." His eyes zigzagged down the freckles on Riley's chest, pausing on the tiny anchor she wore on a chain. Then they dropped to a button she'd realize, only later, had popped undone.

She waited in the car while Noah emptied his locker. As she deleted the photo from his phone, rhythmic messages flashed across the screen:

we can sue
dude no school
she wasn't even that hot

A ladybug trudged up the window. Riley opened it partway, urged the thing outside with a fingernail. She arched her neck back and inhaled the leaden heat. A move, yes. West Virginia. Her brother had called it *idyllic*. That was the word he used, and she supposed that somehow meant *great*. Unbelievable quiet, he'd said last month on the phone. Maybe there she'd sleep.

Since March, she'd awoken in the night with stuffed ears and a tightness clamping her head. She'd see the unmoored cargo ship, *Decisive*, heavy in waters far off Curaçao. How, knot by knot, it pulled itself toward some country in need of cables, or grains, or car parts stored in its rainbow-colored steel containers.

"Weird name for a ship," Noah had said before Dean left for the job.

"Great name." Dean had winked at her. "Perfect in fact."

Perfect, because Dean had been so indecisive about the original assignment. Down at the union hall, there were whispers. Fellow merchant mariners believed the vessel might dock midway in Guantanamo to deliver classified goods. Dean passed the physical, the piss test, the background check and then bailed out, waited for a different hitch, a different ship. "Not going to off-load in that hell and stay deaf. Pretend there ain't screams a mile away. Not helping put weapons in those hands, no sir."

Riley would never forgive his cheap adherence to principle.

Across the school's lawn, students grouped themselves in small constellations. Riley double-checked that the photo was truly deleted and stopped herself from scrolling through prior months. She flipped down her visor and thumbed away smears of mascara. In the mirror, she watched Noah shuffle toward the car. His lanky frame hunched like a septuagenarian over a walker. But once he dumped his bags in the trunk, he slammed it with all the force of an angry fourteen-year-old. Months of rage shook the car.

As Riley pulled out of the parking spot, he stared ahead at a single point on the asphalt.

"It's not right, babe. I'm sorry."

He shut his eyes until they were home.

OVER THE NEXT weeks, Noah said goodbye to his friends, his ball field, his lifelong dentist. He grumbled about Riley inflicting such punishment. He packed his room and, despite a few outbursts, the entire kitchen. He packed his father's belongings, scrawling huge *D*'s on the sides of each box.

"I guess," Riley said, "we'll sort his stuff there."

"Yeah, there."

Noah helped load sold furniture into strangers' trucks, wiping his neck with the navy bandana he now carried everywhere like his father. The house in West Virginia was furnished and money for their old furniture would pay the rent. The first month, at least. Riley quit her job as receptionist at a doctor's office, thrilled to be rid of rude and impatient patients. Lately, if someone had pestered more than twice, she'd smile, urge them back to their seat, then add their details to *Send Me More Info* on religious websites that appeared aggressive in the pursuit of new blood.

During breaks from packing, Noah lay in the yard with his hands clasped on his belly and studied the sky. Sometimes she'd lie beside him. Sometimes she'd start a shanty, hoping he'd join in a round, singing like they did back when they flicked each other with dish-soap hands or a loosely wound towel. Back when Noah ate cookie dough. Now, he ate only the cookies. Beside him on the ground, Riley squinted into the brightness until her vision broke into small orbs.

Noah's stillness scared her these days. The way he blinked less.

Since the school incident, Noah's phone charged in the kitchen each night. Over a Schlitz, she'd thumb through his texts—though it hardly mattered now.

so fucked up. she sent it 1st

Nothing eye-catching. She scrolled up and passed a video of Dean on the back patio. His profile stares off-screen, unaware of the camera. Its jagged zoom soon closes in on his stubble, his dense eyelashes, the scar on his ear. Dean's stare is far and unfamiliar until the camera arcs in front of him, breaking his vacant look. He snaps into a smile. "All right, Spielberg."

Noah giggles behind the camera.

"Enough of that. Come help me fix the—"

Riley tapped the screen still.

THE DRIVE FROM Maryland was only four hours, a swirl through the Alleghenies. Riley held her breath when the trailer hitched to the car pulled into centrifugal force, threatening to tip. When big rigs closed in behind her on the two-lane highway, she squeezed the wheel until her forearms trembled. Pressure filled her ears like a balloon. They burst, as if pricked by a needle, on each downhill. Noah scanned through the radio, lasting ten seconds on each station before he surrendered and pecked away at his phone. His hand rebuffed hers when they reached into the McDonald's bag at the same time, both after the wettest fry. Riley knew she was ripping him from the town where he was born. Maybe they'd get a cat. Perhaps he'd settle for a turtle?

Maybe she'd raise his allowance, somehow. If she could.

Finally, they descended onto a narrow road between slopes

so steep that the trees on both sides bowed, as if to one another. Her brother Mike and his wife had moved into a new house about twenty miles from the place he'd rented for Riley. Mike told her it was "in the zone," whatever that meant. He'd found the rental, signed the lease, set up the utilities, and harassed her for all the paperwork to enroll Noah in school for the following year.

Looks like you think I need a man.

Noah's whole life, Dean had worked four months on board a ship, four off. Having him around was a luxury. A bonus. Sometimes a nuisance. She and Noah knew how to survive quite fine on their own.

Just extra hands. Let people help.

So, she did. She turned the move over to Mike, let him brother her in a way she never had before. The rent was bafflingly cheap, and Riley was grateful. On the phone, he'd tried to tell her about the place—something science-y, about the radiator, maybe. But after a few minutes most of his words drifted by, lost to the foghorn in her skull.

He had a job for her, too. Secretarial. He'd tell her about it when she arrived.

"Jesus fucking Christ," Noah whispered when they stopped at the base of a long driveway. Bright pansies lined the border, their faces upturned like owlets. The brick house at the end had an inordinate number of windows.

"Hey. Clean it up around Uncle Mike, okay?"

When Noah rolled his eyes, Riley pretended not to see. She might fail on allowance, but she could grant this teenage rite. She parked alongside the driveway's entrance, pleased at her forethought to avoid backing out and smashing flowers. Mike appeared in the yard, waved a hairy arm. Flab draped over his belt-cinched shorts and a gold necklace shined out from his collar.

"Welcome, welcome." He squished Riley into a one-armed hug.

Meredith stood in the doorway, wiping her hands with a dish towel. Riley tipped her head and signaled Noah to hug his aunt. "Made stroganoff," Meredith said, with a squeeze of his biceps. The creaminess of the meal seemed heavy for the day's sunshine. Riley felt like she'd swallowed a fist but figured Meredith intended something else with the early dinner. Something kind.

Riley had usually cooked stroganoff on the nights Dean returned home from a stint. It was his favorite, even in hot weather. After a scalding shower that emptied the tank, he and Noah would play chess while she sautéed the beef.

"Getting good, kid," he'd say, then checkmate Noah. When the stroganoff was ready, they'd sit around the table, Noah tripping over piled-up words, cramming four months into one meal. When he paused for a true breath, his noodles were cold. The smell of sizzled mushrooms hung in the air long after the leftovers were stored.

Certain kindnesses, Riley had found, became fragile gifts. She hadn't seen Mike and Meredith since the casket-less memorial.

"Come tour the house." Mike patted Noah's back and guided him inside, which was awash in pale tans—*muted neutrals*, according to Meredith. Fake ivy lolled down from empty bookshelves. Plaques with phrases about faith, family, and food decorated the walls, most in cursive. The place looked more expensive than Riley expected. Mike had been in charge of—was it media operations?—for a local college, filming speakers and weekend ads. But now he'd started something new. Riley wasn't sure what. Meredith stayed home each day, likely keeping all the beige clean. Riley swatted

Noah's hand when he fingered the dried fronds of a cross on the wall. They both gave nods of tired interest to each boasted faucet, each flaunted dimmer.

"Wish we had guest rooms, really do," Mike said as he led them past a long hallway with several closed doors. Meredith cooed in agreement and tucked her sandy bob behind her ears. She'd already asked if Riley wanted a hair appointment, directing the question to Riley's yarmulke of brown roots as if it might accept.

The basement showcased a whole film setup: tripods at varying heights, intricate video cameras, pull-down backgrounds for portraits. Boxes overflowing with clothes lined the walls. A water gun poked out from one. Lights stood tall, cables looped like tails behind them.

"All these puppies," Mike said, gesturing to the entire room with a game-show host's flourish. "Worth more than the house." In the corner, giant monitors and computers sat upon a wide L-shaped desk, along with a messy tower of business cards that Meredith rushed to straighten. "So, this is the office. The studio." He pointed to the desk. "You'll check emails, keep records, mail checks. Stuff like that."

Riley nodded. Easy enough.

"You guys make movies now?" Noah pulled down a neon green background, but it shot up with a whir.

"Sort of. Educational content." Mike's cheeks looked pink and overheated, despite the air-conditioning. He glanced at Meredith, who shook her head. She asked Noah to help brew iced tea upstairs.

Riley sensed Mike waiting, that he expected her to ask something. She didn't. Silence didn't heckle her the way it did others.

And she didn't care what the job was, only that her brother could pay her. Not fire her.

"Want to go over everything next week? Unpack first, all that?"

Riley nodded. She wondered if she could wear sweats to the job but didn't ask.

"You read the house stuff I sent, right?" He led her upstairs. "You ready?"

"Of course." These days, she found herself smiling when she lied, forcing on her most pleasing face, the one most acceptable to others. The rest of her flapped so hard underwater it made her sweat. She hadn't had time to read what he'd sent. There were so many papers, too many—half a ream maybe—in that manila envelope.

Whenever Dean returned from sea, he'd kiss between her brows. "You sure do hold down the fort."

At dinner Riley crunched the stroganoff's underboiled noodles, drained too soon. She vowed to herself to read the papers that night.

Later, in the car, the radio fizzled in and out in spurts. Noah reached in his pocket and removed a business card from the basement desk. She glanced over: *Bespoke Media.* His nimble thumbs flitted over his phone's screen. "Holy shit," he said, then laughed.

"Jesus. Language, Noah."

"Shit." He grinned. "You have to see this website." When Riley exited the highway, Noah held the phone over her lap. The screen blackened. It relit when he tapped it, but whatever he wanted to show her had disappeared. "Man. No service."

Behind them, an antique car honked mere seconds after the light turned green. Noah twisted around and rattled off possible

automakers, searched for its brand. A Buick Skylark, Riley saw.
But she stayed silent, grateful for this puddle of distraction in
which he could splash around.

Signs with u.s. government and private property
streaked by, the text under the headings too dense to catch. They
passed a museum, a phone booth, and a large arrow pointing toward Green Bank as the gauzy light faded into shadows. Hills
overlapped, their tops curving like a braid. Beneath those, smooth
farmland stretched for miles. She pulled over. Thank god Mike had
forced a map on her. Once she had her bearings, Riley returned to
the thin road. Ahead, a tremendous white structure rose from the
horizon. As they drove nearer, it looked more like a colossal satellite dish, the whole thing crosshatched as if made of scaffolding. A
long L-shaped arm, bent like a construction crane, shot out of the
disc's edge and aimed up at the sky. The crane reached as high as
the Washington Monument. Two flashes pulsed at its top. A mist
of rosy light encircled the dish, which could hold football fields.

"Whoa," Noah whispered. Other smaller, imitation discs dotted the fields.

They drove even closer. The contraption sat far back from the
road and was centered on a circle of tan and pristine dirt, like a
supersized pitcher's mound. A high chain-link fence surrounded
the whole thing. Riley turned away from the machine, onto a dirt
path. They jostled toward a weary cabin. The headlights caught
pale regrowth reaching up from splintered trees. In a shallow
marsh, branches jabbed though nets of moss. Light seeped from
the windows of the lone house next door. Its porch teemed with
hoses, crates, and overturned plastic chairs. Cheery decorative
plates hung from the siding, most intact. As Riley parked between

the two houses, a pickup truck with a surplus of antennae pulled in behind her. Its amber siren flung out a series of whoops. A rickety man in a Hawaiian shirt and paint-stained jeans emerged. He left the engine running. Riley's taillights lit the badge pinned to his chest, which gleamed in her rearview mirror. Noah cracked one knuckle, then another.

"It's fine, babe." She locked the doors. "We're fine. Totally fine." Riley inched the window down.

"You the new renters?"

"Yeah, but my brother's the one who—"

"You know you can't drive this thing in here, right?" The man jutted his chin toward their trailer.

"Just for moving in, sorry. Unpacking it tomorrow."

"The car."

"Sorry?"

"Runs on gas. Can't have it here at all. Going to have to tow it out for you in the a.m. at this point." He ignored Riley's confusion and ripped a red sheet off a notepad, stuck it to the home's front door. "Just a warning this time. Cause you're new."

Noah turned on his phone's flashlight. He hovered it over her shoulder as they approached the door to read the harsh capitals:

NRAO INTERFERENCE PROTECTION GROUP
WARNING

VIOLATION OF ORDINANCE ITU-R RA.769 AND ITS MANDATORY PROTECTIONS FOR RADIO ASTRONOMICAL MEASUREMENTS. ALL UNINTENTIONAL RADIATORS ARE FORBIDDEN IN ZONE 1, INCLUDING:

A list ran down the rest of the page, a blank box next to each item. One was checked:

GASOLINE-POWERED MOTOR VEHICLES
(ENGINE SPARK PLUGS PRODUCE RADIOACTIVE INTERFERENCE.)

The words made no sense. Riley read fragments aloud, trying to thread them into meaning. She ground her back teeth together. Since Dean, she'd promised herself not to lose it in front of Noah. So far, she hadn't. When she turned around, she hoped to catch the quack. But the lit-up truck rambled away, receding into a legion of stunted pines.

The house smelled of Windex which, despite its strength, failed to overpower the mildew. Scrapes curved across the floorboards of the open living and kitchen area. A wobbly coffee table sat in front of an olive sofa, a neat array of blankets on one side. The oven looked twice Noah's age. Riley found yogurts and a case of club soda arranged in the fridge. She must thank Meredith tonight before she forgot. She'd never moved into a new place without Dean, without his humming as he double-checked sink hoses, fiddled with the circuit breaker.

Noah was already off-loading boxes. He stacked those with *D*'s into a high tower in the corner, a ripped international postage label still pasted to one's side. The shipping company had mailed items from Dean's cabin—sweatshirts, a few historical novels, and his toothbrush, its bristles wrapped in tissue.

Riley pulled out her cell phone but, like Noah, had no service. A landline hung on the kitchen wall with a curlicue cord that drooped to the floor. As she dialed, Noah took a break and stood beside her. He coiled excess cord around his fingers again and again until his fingertips turned a reddish-purple. *No,* she mouthed, shaking her head as she reached over and undid some of the cord. Mike answered. She thanked him, thanked Meredith, then railed about the Margaritaville gestapo, that crazy loony.

"I told you about the diesel. The telescopes? God, Riley."

She edged away from Noah so he wouldn't hear.

"Three times. Didn't you—? You said you read the stuff. The whole place, that's why it's so cheap."

When Riley hung up, she found the paperwork he'd sent last month. Coffee rings and doodled mazes covered the manila envelope. She sank into the couch. Noah knelt on the floor beside her. They fanned the papers across the table. When she reached for one, she grazed the back of his neck. He, too, hadn't had a haircut since the news of Dean. Shaggy locks covered that telling line where skin met hair—so soft and exact on a boy, only to roughen with age.

The lease noted the property owner as "U.S. Government." A peppy brochure welcomed its reader to Green Bank, part of the 13,000-square-mile National Radio Quiet Zone. Diagrams of circles within circles surrounded pictures of the satellite contraptions and declared them radio telescopes, in bold. They didn't look for stars. They listened for them, detecting their sounds, and searching the places even light failed to reach. Riley scanned a page-long list of rules, then another page of noes. No: microwaves, radio, television broadcasts, cameras, cellular devices, spark plugs, Wi-Fi—all were banned by law.

"Wait. No cell? No Wi-Fi?"

She'd sworn to Noah the move was not a punishment.

"Mom? Come on."

Asterisks dotted a few items: approved dial-up modems, approved devices with protective shields and, only in outer zones, approved microwaves. She remembered, just then, a phone call with Mike and his description of the enormous touchy machines, during which she'd carved split-open Oreos into phases of the moon with her fingernail.

"It's like a candle in total darkness," he'd said. "Our eyes, they say, can see that flickering a mile away. A mile. All of a sudden, you shine a spotlight? Candle disappears."

She'd lined up the cookies in order as he rambled, waxing to waning.

"Those sounds up in the stratosphere the telescopes find? They're so weak—any other signals drown them right out."

After she'd eaten her work, she dreamt of a distant burning dot. Then the floodlight that erased it from view.

Now, in their new home, Noah reread the brochure several times before resting his forehead on the table's edge. "Mike has freaking Wi-Fi. Can't we just live with them?"

"No room." She forced a smile.

"Sure." He glanced again at the brochure.

"It's not forever, Noah."

"There's no way," he said, before huffing off to the shower.

His phone was plugged in across the room. Riley tapped it to life. As she opened the texts, someone banged on the front door. "Dealing with the stupid car tomorrow, okay?" she yelled, not wanting the guard's flashlight in her face again. "Diesel. I get it." After another series of knocks, she cursed the man, then answered.

But a squat woman in a frayed teal robe stood outside, barefoot.

Her hair hung in limp, gray pigtails. The light bounced off her glasses, made it hard to see her eyes.

"Turn it off. You have to turn it off." She splayed her fingers as if showing off a manicure. "See? Already they're swelling."

Riley said nothing, wondered where one could buy beer.

The woman pointed at the phone Riley held. "Please."

Unsure what else to do, Riley slid the phone in her back pocket.

"Electrosensitives, we're called." The woman repositioned her glasses farther up her nose. "Rashes, chest pain, trouble speaking—you name it. Doctors don't much believe us, but it's a dang jackhammer to the head."

Riley was grateful for the landline, 911 within easy reach.

"Got so bad, tried putting Faraday cages around the culprits. You know, shields? Block those frequencies. But this old body, well, it still shrieked if anyone fired up a TV. Left Pittsburgh, left my bakery, moved here, got gas lamps."

Feet padded down the hallway behind Riley. A door slammed.

"My kid, sorry." Why she apologized to this fretful stranger, she didn't know.

"Lookie there. Thought the old cat had your tongue." The woman tried to peer through the doorway, but Riley blocked her view.

"Anyway, even looked into a repurposed space suit, so I could leave the house, not feel the pain. But they're oodles of dollars. Heard about this place three years ago, and it's the only place I don't."

"Don't what?'

"Don't feel the pain. I'm Kit by the by."

A sliver of robe slipped open. Riley sensed Kit was naked underneath. The revealed skin looked like crumpled-up paper, flattened anew.

"So, we got the three types here—telescopers, us, and the folk whose folks have been here long as the land. Which are you?"

"Don't know."

Kit inspected Riley's face then turned away. She walked back to the house next door, navigating patches of mud with heavy side-steps as if she wore the pined-for space suit. "I know it's still on. Don't think I can't feel it."

Before Riley turned off the phone, she saw Noah's most recent text: *holy shit guys my uncle makes porn.* Thankfully, *Not Delivered* and a red exclamation point accompanied his words.

That night, Riley dreamt again of a distant circle, orange and aglow. Her own shallow breaths woke her, the gasps loud in the stillness.

IT WASN'T PORN. Not exactly. Or at least not always, she'd discover when she began work the next week. They were "customs." Go ahead, ask for anything. Mike and Meredith set a price, contacted their actors, then produced the video. Their website gloated they'd fill any and all requests, which was true, mostly. If they didn't like the vision or it was violent, they trashed the email, pretended it never came through.

"Market's saturated with the normal stuff," Mike said. "People are immune. Some, anyway. Takes something unique, that they're shy about maybe, to make them feel—"

Riley didn't care. He let her wear sweats and Meredith usually sent her home with two plates of pale tan food.

Each morning she'd unroll the windows on the diesel clunker

that Mike helped her buy on trade. She'd back out past Kit's car, which never went anywhere. Its tires had sunk into the ground. Torn bumper stickers, plastered atop each other, covered the backside. Their rectangles reminded Riley of bright, stacked shipping containers. She never asked Dean but assumed loud colors equaled visibility. After she pulled onto the road, she'd speed through the valley where air from the open window dried her tears.

As promised, the job was easy—a lot of loading and unloading for scenes shot on location, a lot of records, a lot of emails. At the start and end of each day, she called out requests to Mike, one by one. While he fixed lights or edited videos, he'd set prices.

"Rubbing mayo through hair?"

"Standard."

"Squishing a bug with a loafer?"

"Standard. No, plus fifty for karma."

"Burning a stamp collection?"

"Fire. Plus four hundred."

Sometimes, she fielded prickly messages from clients who felt cheated, that the product wasn't right. "She was supposed to be pinched on the elbow, not the upper arm." Sometimes Riley opened florid and effusive thank-yous, paragraphs more suited for therapy. And whenever performers arrived, she would excuse herself and flip through tabloids in the kitchen, uninterested in the shape of others' secrets.

After one Wednesday of Slinkys and ice-baths, she scrolled through emails, ready for the typical call-and-response. There was one sent at 3:22 p.m., no subject. Riley read through twice, unsure how to summarize it for Mike.

Hi. wondering how much it would cost to have someone a woman
I guess say really close to the camera, say nothing's that bad, or
gonna stay bad, or your fault. Or this is the place for you. Or
something like that maybe I don't know. maybe just say it a lot.
Doesn't need to be naked or nothing just asking how much. thx

The sender's address was only jumbled letters and numbers. Riley read the note aloud, verbatim.

"Standard."

She was careful in her reply, double-checked her spelling. "Don't you think it's a touch . . . I don't know."

In one hand Mike held a bag of charcoal and a feather duster. In the other, a knee brace and chocolate sauce. He shrugged.

Riley wanted to add a tender extra to the reply. Something uplifting, perhaps. But Mike crossed behind her, impatient for more messages.

When she returned home, Noah wasn't there but his phone was—plugged in and encased in some silver mesh bag. She removed it, turned it on. His chessboard lay open on the table, both sides mid-game. There was only one message from that morning, outgoing and undelivered, offset by the red exclamation.

WV sux. can't take this place anymore- its like amish

Her mouth went dry. She should have brought him to Mike's each day instead of leaving him alone here, a place that even birds avoided. There was a café in an outer zone with guarded, nosy locals, who'd likely offer puncturing opinions about his all-day presence. Why hadn't she learned chess? She'd tried, but still.

"Noah?" He was without his phone, his useless phone. Riley

checked his room and called for him again. She hadn't raised his allowance, hadn't bought a turtle.

Outside, laughter overlapped, followed by the back-and-forth wheeze of a saw. In front of Kit's porch, Noah bent over a plank while she supervised. Sweat soaked the back of his T-shirt.

Riley covered her nose and mouth so as not to inhale the mist of rising sawdust.

"Figured you were home when these puppies got all swole," said Kit. She waggled her fingers in the air and scowled. She was, as usual, in her robe.

Noah wiped his forearms with his bandana. "Helping make a giant Faraday cage. For the electromagnetic waves?"

Riley shook her head. "For the electro—"

"Signal hits, electrons in the metal realign to an opposite charge, and boom! Cancel it out. Building one around her house."

"Whole place." Kit's glasses had darkened into sunglasses which she tilted down, revealing her eyes so she could scan the road. "Cars drive through, radios still scanning. Idiots don't know there's nothing for them out here."

"Mom, you know the telescopes? They're so sensitive they can hear a snowflake hit the ground."

Kit leaned against a dent on her car. "You're on Neptune and your phone's even on, they hear it."

"A lot of phones on Neptune?" Riley asked.

Noah sighed.

She tried again. "Telescopes ever hear anything?"

Kit said nothing. Instead, she reached for Riley's necklace and scrutinized the small anchor. "Not yet."

Riley put her hand over Kit's, removing it from the chain.

That night, as she slept, Riley's ears filled as they always did in a sudden altitude shift. Tentacles of kelp on the ocean floor encircled the body before it swirled up, pulled by a funnel that spit it back through the surface—the thunk of a head, maybe a knee, against the ship's keel—all rewinding to the ripples that first pooled around the warm and un-sunk body. Rewinding to the splash. Then the hole. Always a hole. Always a filmstrip with one darkened square: Dean at the railing. Leaning, perhaps. Flicking cigarette ash into the sea. He'd be in filthy coveralls, a hard hat maybe, or maybe mussed hair, and weeks' worth of softening stubble that would have scraped her chin. In pictures—he'd sent so many pictures—there were three railings.

The highest stood level with his heart.

But there was no body, only the blank, dark square filled with freak accidents and failed organs. Something inside him perhaps shut down. So many nights, she'd held his novels by their spines and shaken them, but nothing ever fell out.

THE NEXT MORNING, Noah was in Kit's yard before break-fast, drilling large veils of metal net into wood. Kit watered the plants that had fallen prostrate over her porch's edge. Riley set a box of granola bars by the toolbox. Noah said something she couldn't hear, and Kit threatened him with the hose. Noah's buoy-ant laughter belonged on a playground. So did Kit's. Neither of them glanced at Riley's car as it pulled away.

At Mike's, she hustled downstairs instead of lingering over her usual mug of weak coffee and awkward smiles with Meredith, smiles that dared the other to fold. Riley searched the inbox for the jumbled email address. Still no response. No response that evening nor the day after that. When she asked Mike if they should reach out, he chided her. "We only respond, and we responded."

Over a belated cup of coffee, she spoke to Meredith about the note.

"A lot of our business is minding it, Riley."

"Tell that to my neighbor." She tugged at the pilled fabric of her sweats.

Meredith stayed silent until Riley's eyes lifted and found hers. "You ever scream?"

Riley brushed the picked-at bits to the floor. "At Noah?"

"No. What kind of mother—" Meredith dampened a paper towel, cleaned the wood floor by Riley's feet. "I mean get in the car where no one can hear you and scream 'til you're out of air."

"You do that?"

Meredith cleared away their half-full mugs. "Only saw it on a talk show. Supposed to help."

Figured. Hard to see her eking out a yowl. "Just one more message, in case?"

Mike overheard and shouted from the hallway. "Leave it, Riley. Not up to us to chase after reasons."

At night, she listened for the steady in-and-out of Noah's fuzzy snore. Riley couldn't stop picturing the sender typing the note, thick pointer finger by finger. She placed him in different rooms, unpuzzling the possibilities of things gone wrong. Though she tried to contain him to an imagined house, he always ended up at the railing. Greedy black waters below. She'd called the shipping company, talked to the captain even. She called again. But each time, all they revealed was he'd been on break. A watch stander heard the splash, saw the ripples, dispatched the rescue. It returned empty. They were sorry—so, so sorry.

ON THE TENTH day without a response, Riley emailed.

We'll do it for free. Please be in touch.

She didn't tell Mike, figured he could take it out of her check.

That evening, the telescope brimmed with pink light. How it repositioned itself, and at what times, she didn't know. Never saw. When she returned from work, the Margaritaville guard was sweating alongside Noah, raising posts to cover Kit's roof. Noah steadied the ladder while the man climbed high to hammer in more armor of metal netting. Riley sat on her doorstep and nursed a beer. She worried about Noah's strength, his wispy arms unprepared for a grown man's fall. Kit's hands stayed glued to her hips as she issued orders. Her upturned nose followed every hammer strike. Sometimes, she'd yell to Riley who didn't hear the words but lifted her can, toasting a cheers anyway.

Later, over Meredith's plates of tuna casserole, Noah bubbled with statistics: efficacy, distance, percentages. His words floated away. After he went to bed, Riley turned on his phone, opened the texts and searched for attempts. She found none. He'd stopped. Surrendered to this place. Or learned to delete them, she supposed. On the couch, she hugged a cushion to herself and found the last video of Dean. Riley squeezed the worn fabric as she watched the few seconds. After the eleventh play, the screen froze right before he realizes Noah's there with the camera. Before his *all right, Spielberg.* She thought she knew all Dean's faces, but this one was foreign. The stiffness in his eyes, the sunken corners of his lips. She shook the phone, trying to make the picture disappear. The image remained. She turned the phone off and when she looked up, Noah stood in the hall. He said nothing.

THE NEXT MORNING'S rain clung to the mesh shielding that now encased Kit's house. As Riley left for work, she saw Kit and Noah on the porch. Both held teacups aloft. They waved, wide and high, as if from afar. Noah pushed through a flap in the mesh. "You like it?"

"Quite the eyesore. Think it works?"

Before he could answer, Kit hollered, asked if she wanted tea. She did not.

Nor did she want Meredith's weak coffee. Riley sat at the computer until lunch, rereading the note, clicking refresh. No response. That evening, still nothing. She left with a Tupperware bowl full of macaroni salad. But instead of starting the car, she sat with the chilly plastic on her thighs. She dropped her forehead to the wheel and tried to scream, but nothing more than a stilted *aaah* escaped, like the doctor's depressor flattened her tongue. Ridiculous, this cure. Plus, they might hear. *Not that bad, not gonna stay bad, not your fault.* She grabbed a blanket from the trunk, then returned inside.

"Forgot something. Sorry!" A sugary votive burned at dinnertime, like a mouth might mistake scent for taste. Muffled acknowledgment came from the back dining room. Unseen, Riley hurried to the basement. She grabbed a bulky video camera and folded tripod, swaddling the blanket around the equipment. On the balls of her feet, she crept up the stairs and scurried out the door. Before it clicked shut, Meredith appeared.

"What'd you forget?"

Riley didn't turn. Instead, she wriggled her torso, hoping the blanket undid itself so her haul looked less secretive. "Mike said Noah could borrow some stuff."

"Hey, Mike?" Even her yell was thin.

"Please."

Meredith arced around Riley, faced her. "Does he know how to use it?"

"What do you think?"

Mike's footsteps and mutters of *middle of dinner* grew closer.

"Accidents happen, you know." Meredith pursed her dry lips.

"Come on, Mer." Riley looked past her and repositioned the blanket. "Please."

Meredith studied the goods Riley held. "It's nothing," she called, before pulling the door shut behind her. "Hope he only needs it one night. That way Mike certainly can't miss it." She raised her penciled-in brows. "One night."

Riley nodded, overwhelmed by the urge to hug Meredith, yet relieved the load in her arms prevented it.

At home, Riley set up the tripod in the living room, screwed in the camera. She brushed her hair into a loose ponytail, changed from her T-shirt into a sleeveless shell, the color of daffodils, and even shaved her armpits. Not her legs. She'd shoot waist-up, so the sweatpants stayed. She powered the camera, hit record. As Riley backed against the living room wall, she took a breath, puffed it into her cheeks. The words. What to say. *Not that bad, not gonna stay bad, not your fault.* She began. A high-pitched screech interrupted.

Noah barged into the house. "Jesus, Mom. Stop." He shut off the camera, squinted at her as though she were a dog in need of housebreaking. "Kit can feel that."

"In that fortress?" Riley chuckled. All that metal, all that time. "Too bad."

"Don't be a bitch."

The word struck like a match, illuminating an unbearable thought, a Loch Ness monster of a thought—one others, better others, could pretend out of existence. Pretend away. But there it rose, looming: She hated his hair, hated his eyelashes, the way his wrists hyperflexed. Any part of him that was Dean's, she hated. Hated him for having it, holding it, stealing it. Noah kept a bit of Dean forever. Not her. He was water gone through her cupped, now drying, hands. Noah would sleep and wake with permanent, unforgivable souvenirs, while Dean's boxes would dwindle one by one to the trash, weekend by weekend to the thrift store, emptying the corner he still held, until he was no longer a part of this place.

Another shriek pealed outside the window. Somehow, impossibly, decibels louder.

Riley turned the camera back on. Bile rose in her throat. She searched Noah for traces of herself but found only Dean. "Doctors don't—actual doctors don't believe in this shit. It's in that woman's head, okay?"

He squeezed his eyes closed in response, Dean's curly lashes on display.

"Whatever she thinks she has, Noah, it doesn't exist."

"Prove it." Again, he turned off the video camera.

The allegiance pierced her. Neither moved as they stared at each other. Riley willed herself not to back down her usual moment-too-soon, though he'd think less of her either way. They stared until her eyes grew watery and his outline wavered, and Riley saw herself, tiny as a pencil tip in his pupil. She broke first, dropped her gaze to his beautiful wrist. After a moment, she shouldered past him and undid the camera. She hoisted the equipment, wrestled with the door, and tramped outside as night unspooled from the hills.

"Hey, it's pitch-black out there," Noah called from the open doorway. "What are you doing?"

With each step, mud spurted up the calves of her sweatpants.

"Mom?"

Riley crossed the empty road.

"Mom, come on. Come back."

Her nose ran. She tried to wipe it, but her arms were too full. An unexpected chill tightened her shoulders as she waded into the thick silence—no crickets, no owls, no cars. No breeze either as though that, too, gave wide berth to the machines. She walked a rigid line, not sure how far was far enough, until she reached the vapory glow of the telescope and its base encircled by the well-groomed sand, all chained in by fence. Along it, signs with slashed circles forbade entry and all electronics. She stabbed the tripod's feet into the wet dirt.

After Riley attached the camera, she turned it on—then off and on a few more times, hoping its radio-magnetic-electro-whatevers somehow doubled in power next to the telescope and that Kit indeed felt the jolts. A red button blinked as she stepped backward, recording. Her eyes fixed on the dot. "Hi." Her whisper cracked. She cleared her throat. *Say really close.*

Riley forgot the exact words but started to speak, her voice trembling and open in the quiet. Her words spilled out faster. She didn't see the telescope behind her pop with light, or the flashes that skittered like gravel over its cupped center. She couldn't know what sounds, what echoes beyond light's reach, the telescope grasped, or that the swollen heave of the machine's rotation and its searching tilt drowned out her voice. As Riley spoke, she inched toward the camera. She didn't see Kit emerge from her metal veil or drop her hands from her ears. She didn't hear Noah, out of breath, approach with his uncharged phone which he angled at the tremendous disc before panning the sky. She didn't stop talking, stepping even closer to the lens as insistent flashes from the telescope multiplied behind her. She also didn't remember the video camera's empty slot. She hadn't checked for a memory card so didn't know the night, and whatever it heard, would escape uncaptured. She didn't see the guard in his Hawaiian shirt or hear him slam the truck door, his Maglite grazing over her to aim, instead, at the camera's blinking red dot.

Lara Hughes holds an MFA in fiction from Vanderbilt University. Her writing has received support from the New York State Summer Writers Institute and appeared as an Emerging Writer's Prize winner in *The Arkansas International*. She currently lives in Nashville, where she is at work on a novel and short story collection.

Editor's Note

What first struck me about "A Resting Place" were the details: a fleshy tarp, a pinched olive, a dog with a sloppy tongue, a man named Gorm. Celine Ipek's writing is entirely assured—spare, painterly, sneakily sharp and sneakily funny. She polishes the surface to a sheen that reveals the cracks lurking below. Over the course of the story, she patiently pries those cracks open, exposing a current of class, aspiration, and the slippery boundary between self-improvement and self-erasure.

At the center is Alice, our hesitant guide through a world that seems certain how she should feel, move, rest, love. The story never tells us how to feel about her—or anyone, really—but in its restraint and precision, it gradually reveals how much we're all shaped by longing, performance, and proximity to power. A quietly unsettling account of being a person in a body, trying to figure out how to live.

Eli Horowitz, Guest Editor
McSweeney's Quarterly

A Resting Place

Celine Ipek

THE WOMAN. THE PASTURE. THE DRY WIND AND THE brightening hills. The cypresses, thin-branched and narrow. The woman. She wore only a white cotton shirt, unbuttoned in the front, loose around her breasts.

The woman. Sylvia. She greeted Alice and Tom outside, wrapped them in her arms. Welcome, she said, a hand in Alice's hair. Welcome, she said, and took Tom's bag, lifting it over her shoulder before he could protest. Sylvia asked about their train ride, as she led them to the villa. She asked about their marriage. They weren't married, Alice said. How wonderful, Sylvia said, to arrive so open. When they reached the door, she turned. She had them breathe deeply. She had them repeat: *I am taking time for the sacred. I am blessed by rest.*

At home, Alice used unscented face creams. She cycled to her office and avoided the man urinating outside. Tom slept in long after Alice left. He liked to tell people he worked with his hands. By this, he meant he worked in digital currency. Alice and Tom lived in a beautiful apartment. They had beautiful spoons and knives and a heavy gold mirror from an estate sale. Tom found many things at estate sales. Sets of wooden picture frames and jackets with one-button cuffs. He once gave Alice a slip dress the color of steamed milk. It's real silk, he told her, and she thought the dress might be ugly and not made of real silk, but she put it on.

Sylvia served dinner on dimpled stoneware. Bread warmed with oil, filled with grapes. Slabs of meat, thick-skinned tomatoes. There were four other guests on the retreat, and they all gathered around Sylvia's table. Alice sat opposite Tom, working her teeth around the raw patch of skin in her cheek. Tom had brought her here. Tom, who had hired a mind-and-body healer named Gorm after his mother died. Tom, who had carefully charted his food intake and gained muscle, who had prepared bowls of ice water and dunked his face like an ostrich.

The other guests came from cities with glass bridges, towns in the foothills of mountains. Some didn't come from any one place. They crossed bone-stark strips of sand, slept on granite islands. They had pushed-back cuticles and soft elbows. Tom was not so different from them. He grew up with built-in bookshelves, a separate pantry. He had a dog with a sloppy tongue, and a second house, on the coast. When Alice met him, she was wary. She had lived next to a cornfield as a child, had lived among run-down school buses and pamphlets of choir songs. Then she moved far from her cornfield and worked in a cubicle. She did a lot of waiting, with her legs neatly crossed. She uncapped expensive pens and answered different phones. One moment, please, she'd say, smiling and thinking of sagging skin and tiny fluorescent lights.

There was sweet almond paste and semolina cake for dessert. Sylvia began talking about a lover, fingering the pendant at her neck as she spoke. Once, she said, the lover had brought her to a southern country with ceramic roofs and tangerine juice. He brought her to basilicas with rose windows and he undressed her on the terrace of their hotel room. The older woman beside Alice had been to the same country. Had Sylvia gone to that museum? That museum with the scrap-metal sculptures? No, Sylvia had not. She had been too busy fucking and eating and swimming. Alice was the first to rise from the table—the loud scrape of her chair against the floor. The other guests looked away. Once they looked away, they couldn't stop looking away. Thank you so much, Alice said. Sweat collected beneath her underarms. I might go to bed, Alice said. She wanted cold lotion on her eyelids. She wanted one of the pills she hid in her suitcase. She wanted room-temperature water.

Alice's room overlooked the pool built at the back of the villa. The setting sun pearled the horizon, and houses shaped like cubes dotted the hills. Alice stripped off her clothes and turned on the faucet. There was a cluster of shells in the sink, spiraling conches and calico clams, and Alice picked them up and held them to her ear. She imagined nicking her finger on the sharp edges and bloodying the sink, imagined Sylvia having to fish more shells from the water and arrange them in a pile all over again. There were many things Alice worried about. She worried about the spot in her mouth that sometimes ached and sometimes didn't. She worried about knocking into people in fancy rooms. She worried about the child she always saw with the urinating man outside her office. She worried about going to bed alone. Then she finished washing her hands and didn't nick her finger.

In the morning, Alice found Tom sitting by a potted plant in the kitchen. Two of the other guests were passing a joint. They wore loose-fitting garments, had their blond hair tied back with ribbons. Alice wondered if they might be sisters. When she asked, they laughed. They were not sisters. They were in love. Then they coughed in her face. Where are the others? Alice said to Tom. Hard to tell, Tom said. The potted plant was very green, and he dug his finger into the soil. There was a sunrise hike, one of the ribboned lovers said. To the birthing grove, the other said. Oh, Alice said. There aren't any rules here, Tom said, and he inspected the soil under his nails, and Alice accepted the joint from the ribboned lovers.

There was a recurring dream Alice had, a dream of a yellowing field and a great big tree. Beneath the tree was all of Alice and Tom's furniture from their apartment. Their firm spring mattress, their little gas oven. Their chandelier, suspended from a branch. Their woolly blanket and all their spoons and knives.

Should she tell Tom this? Alice wasn't sure.

Babe, Tom said, I'm pretty high.

Alice once posted a series of pictures of herself online, and waited. When men complimented her, she wrote to them. *Your arms are so big. Your head is so round. You look good. You look so good. You look so special today.* Alice knew she was not supposed to be doing things like this anymore. She read the men's messages, then called Tom and brought him a whole chicken and a puffy flower. That night he pinched her nipples and said things like: Are you going to be good for me? Of course she was.

The sunrise hikers returned, stepping toward the pool, extending their arms above their heads. They were breathless and beaming. They had walked in honeyed light, had seen goats and churches and tractors. Tractors? Alice said. The birthing grove was exquisite, a guest said. Just exquisite. He wore chino shorts and leather boots. Soon Sylvia disappeared inside and came back out with a shawl draped over her shoulders. She carried a fluted pitcher, a tray of olives and pistachios. Alice ate pistachios all the time in her office, purchased them in individually wrapped calorie packs. I eat these all the time, she said. The other guests reached for thin-stemmed chalices and took off their shoes. The ribboned lovers, in crocheted swimsuits, floated on their backs. Tom reclined on a chaise lounge. The man in chino shorts spat an olive pit into his palm.

There was a serious bird problem, the man in chino shorts explained. He had been holding another olive between his fingers for a while, and Alice wondered when he'd eat it. A serious, serious problem, he said. He was an architect of many-storied buildings, and birds kept careening into his windows. So horrible, the older woman said. Is it fatal? Tom asked. The architect was pained. My windows, he said.

There was a time when Alice had had a slanted, windowless room and a cabinet full of oval sleeping tablets the color of cranberries. This was when she had first moved away from her cornfield. There were game shows she watched at night. There were polyester skirts she ironed. There was a lamp she kept by her bed, a lamp with an oiled brass base and a milk glass shade. Once, she'd turned on her lamp and peeled a hard-boiled egg and watched her show. A man in a suit was tallying the amount of edible furniture in a house. He bit into a calendar made of sugar and a pillow made of dough and a desk made of metal. Sometimes the furniture was just furniture.

I am blessed by rest. I am taking time for the sacred. I am birthing myself, over and over. They were by the pool's edge. Alice pulled hairs from her calves and let them drift off while Tom and the other guests copied Sylvia's movements. Tom was right by Sylvia, his shirt off. His knees were spread wide, his forehead touching the ground. He said: I am blessed. I am birthing myself. You are, Sylvia said. She seemed proud, moving Tom's head to her lap. Alice watched Sylvia's hands press into his scalp.

Alice watched Sylvia's hands and wondered whether it would be easy to get into bed with the architect. He was so serious about the birds—no, not the birds, but his windows. How much could his projects cost? The other guests had lost Sylvia's guidance, but the architect kept going, bending his elbows and bringing his thumbs to the back of his neck. Alice could lower her mouth onto the furry stretch of his belly. Alice could marry him, and the architect could say: Here is my wife. She is young and I know her well. Alice could say: I am his wife. I am young and easy to get to know. She could say: Look at my husband's windows. They are well made and definitely not a danger to wildlife.

Before they left for Sylvia's, Alice and Tom had hosted an evening gathering for their friends. They would be gone for only a week, but Tom wanted their friends to miss them, so Alice had agreed. Their friends brought pale-berried tarts, natural wine with children's drawings on the label. They draped their brightly colored scarves on Alice and Tom's couch. They kissed Alice's cheek and complimented the new chandelier. Their friends said: You're really going! Alice's friend joked: You're letting him sleep with that woman, Alice? Alice drank organic wine and felt it stain her teeth. After everyone left, she lit rosemary-scented candles and drew a bath. Tom came in, touched her shoulders, and rinsed her scalp. Why are you friends with her? he said. Alice took his hand

and traced the crease in her hips, the faint scar on her knee. She pointed at their beautiful apartment and all their beautiful things. He'd forgiven her, Tom said, hadn't he?

I am blessed by rest. I am taking care of my path. I am taking care. There was a fleshy tarp on the ground, a spread of mirrors. The ribboned lovers held hands and circled their reflection. The older woman smoothed the backs of her heels. The architect touched the glass in front of him, touched the curve of his shoulders and the spot of acne on his jaw. Tom lay on his back, baring his gums, bringing a compact to his teeth. They should play, Sylvia was saying. They should see their limbs as children.

Sylvia pulled Alice into a corner. Alice wasn't playing, she said. Why wasn't Alice playing? I am, Alice said. I'm trying to. I want to help you, Sylvia said. A shadow stretched across the half-timbered ceiling, across the painting of a bloated cloud.

Tom was still attending to his teeth, and the hours were still passing. Alice wanted to ask whether she was taking care. Alice wanted to ask whether she was running late. Instead, she poked at a split end. She chewed her cheek. Alice must not be meditating enough, Sylvia said. She should meditate and she should sit. One summer, I sat all the time, Sylvia said. I sat and sat in a room that smelled of a garden. Okay, Alice said.

There had been Alice's broken stove and Alice's cheap work shoes and Alice's stuffed-up nose and there had been Tom's strong-lined fireplace and Tom's unwrinkled friends. If Tom could love me, Alice would say as she scrubbed her wrists, if Tom could love me. Then Tom loved her. Then she threw out her cigarettes and she kissed two strangers at a different stranger's party and she left her things in her smoke-stained hallway.

The guests sheltered under striped parasols, kneaded oil into their chests. They waded into the water and used towels hemmed with lace and wrote in notebooks with sewn pages. They dried laundry with pins and rope. They soaped porcelain plates in the sink. They polished all the surfaces and when they were done they sat outside and admired their hard work. They had done so well, Sylvia said. They were harnessing—harnessing something. They were harnessing and releasing. The guests nodded. They had never felt so attuned.

One day Alice stood in the kitchen with a dry cloth, the droplets from a colander wetting her sleeve. Tom washed and she wiped and the architect opened cabinets. The ribboned lovers lay out beneath the sun. They had never seen their fathers pray in grasslands beneath a heating sky, had never been slapped in a lot behind a laundromat. None of them, Alice thought. Now she was with them in this place. She was filling saltshakers and fixing turned-up carpet corners and Tom was paying for them to do so and soon she would board another plane and there would be room, room, room. She would stretch her legs as far as she could and there would still be room.

I am taking time for the sacred. I am filling my body with light. I am filling my body. It was their final night. On Sylvia's table: A vase of laurels, a jug of cherry absinthe. A ring of waxed cheese. Sylvia had asked Alice to sit by her, and Alice could feel the up-and-down of Sylvia's leg. She'd been married once, Sylvia was saying, a long time ago. Her husband had been a good man. He'd kept a stack of cassette tapes in his car. He trimmed his beard. He sold custom suits, measuring the shoulders of rich men and richer men and using the bathrooms in their plaster-columned houses. Now he was far away, she said. There was butter on Alice's thumb, and she reached for her napkin beneath the table.

Then Tom was telling them about his second house, on the coast. God, he said, God, he couldn't believe how good it was. He missed his mother, he said. He missed his mother and he missed the coast. The architect was curious. Did Tom remember the square footage of that house? It was raised on stilts, wasn't it? Sylvia was curious. Did Tom's family rely on the ferry schedule? She used to live in a beach town, had worried about planning clambakes and boat rides. She had kept a chart of the moon and tides by her bed.

Then Sylvia turned. Then Sylvia asked: Had Alice been to Tom's second house?

Alice had not been to Tom's second house. I'm not too sure why, she said, and she drank from her cup. She said: I'm not too sure about a lot of things. She said: I've never met Tom's mother and I've never had a sibling or a baby. She said: Sometimes I make terrible faces in the mirror, as if I'm possessed, and sometimes I make terrible faces at the ceiling when Tom is fucking me, when Tom can't see my face and I can't see either one of us. Sometimes I pretend I'm in my windowless room, and if I died no one would know for years, and that wouldn't be so bad, would it? I thought it might be bad, but—it wouldn't be.

Alice was out of breath. There was a divot between Sylvia's brows, and the divot was deepening. She seemed older than before. She seemed tired and old. The makeup beneath her eyes pilled. The slope of her nose was dry. The gem at her neck was dull. Alice pictured herself snapping it off, then felt her hand moving. The pendant was in her fist, sharp against her palm. The butter on her finger was the butter on the pendant. Alice, said Sylvia.

Alice, said the architect. Alice, said Tom, Alice, that isn't yours, and Tom's voice was suddenly a voice Alice had never known. Tom's face was suddenly the face of a stranger's. Alice placed the pendant in her mouth. She could almost imagine the thickness of dough. She could almost imagine. Thank you, she said, and she stayed in her chair.

The woman. The guests. The checkerboard floors, all the polished surfaces. The kettle, steaming and full. The easel, propped up by a doorway that wasn't a doorway. The guests. They went on walks and dove into the pool and used dollops of cream from clear vials. They talked about returning to monasteries and making love. They talked about a drowned couple and the opera. In the evenings, they were clean as linen. They were blessed by rest. They sat beneath a spill of stars and ate giant white fish and left all the bones.

Celine Ipek was born in 1999 and lives in Brooklyn, New York. Her fiction has appeared in *McSweeney's Quarterly*. She teaches in the writing department at Columbia University.

Editor's Note

The first thing I notice about Jessie Li's "Mouth and Heart" is its austere yet vivid imagery, conjuring a world that's both everyday and strange: "a bowl of sunny green pears," "pages scalloped with bug bites," "a mop of rough plastic filaments." But the story's real power comes from how it interrogates the desire to be extraordinary. At the story's center, a daughter struggles with dislocation and rage alongside the toll of her father's academic compromise: "He had been a postdoctoral fellow for my entire life." In spite of her fury, she sees her father, a Chinese immigrant, with tenderness and nuance, his love expressed not in grand gestures but in small, exacting words of care. Li's story is about what it means to be estranged, to want, and to come into understanding too late for it to change anything. It lingers in the imagination with a lasting ache.

Paul Lisicky, Editor
StoryQuarterly

Mouth and Heart

Jessie Li

MY FATHER IS A SIMPLE MAN.

When I was in high school, he came to cheer for me at a cross-country race. It was October and raining, a torrential and unforgiving downpour that turned the hills into a sludge that I climbed, with muddied hands and knees, while water soaked into my shoes and softened my toes. The course was three-point-one miles—five kilometers—and after I had passed the first mile marker, scrambling up one of those big slushy hills, my father emerged, standing on the sidewalk, under a bright yellow umbrella. He looked alien, a burst of color before the gray sky.

I broke into a smile, blinking through the rain, and gave him a big wave.

But he shook his head. "Don't run too fast!" he shouted. "It's okay if you can't finish!"

I stopped waving. I pumped my arms faster and tipped my head back until the rain rippled down my throat.

That was the first and last race he watched me run.

IN CHINA, MY father had studied geology, which was why we didn't attend the Chinese Baptist church across the main road from our neighborhood, in the suburbs of Virginia. The earth was four and a half billion years old, my father said, so there was no reason we should believe in scriptures that denied that. But there was something to learn from the stories of Jesus. A poster of the Golden Rule hung on the wall of my room, its letters flecked with glitter, which fell over my pillow and left shining spots in my hair when I woke.

My mother had died when I was born, a loss which struck me as strange only when I started elementary school and realized that everyone else had two parents, and each parent had been assigned a role—the mother was the one who bought your school supplies, and the father was the one whose job you bragged about during recess.

I had no choice but to lie about my life.

"My house has a swimming pool," I announced one day in the cafeteria.

Sophie and her best friend Violet sat across from me. I knew Violet from Chinese School, where she was regarded as cool. She wore clothing from Abercrombie & Fitch, and I coveted her teal drawstring dress, with the fuchsia moose embroidered on the chest.

Violet was eating apple sticks; the red skins glistened under the fluorescent lights.

"That's not true," she said.

"It is," I insisted. "My father built it, and there are flowers growing all around—"

I paused to remember the names of flowers.

"—daisies and pansies and hydrangeas," I said, satisfied with the last one. "You'll see when you come to my birthday party, it's so big, it's bigger than the basketball court."

My birthday was in July, so they would never know.

Sophie leaned forward, and cast a knowing look at Violet. "What about your mom?"

"My mom's dead." I laughed. "She was racing a horse. She won, and then it threw her off."

I had been reading a series about a girl who was in love with a horse. I felt sorry for the picture on the kitchen shelf, in a ceramic frame with chipped roses, where my mother, whose face was the size of my thumb, lived suspended in time. She wore a knee-length dress, puffed at the shoulders, and clutched a red bouquet. My father, wearing a suit, wrapped one arm around her waist. I had never seen him wear a suit in real life.

"My mom said your family's poor," Violet said. "So you can't have a pool."

Sophie let out a shriek. I thought she might come to my rescue, but she was laughing.

My arms turned hot. "Can too," I said, and stuck my tongue out, and ate my chicken filet sandwich.

The truth was that nobody ever came to our house. As a result, I believed adults didn't have friends, and only other children did. It was a reassurance that eventually I would grow old and it would be acceptable to be a loner.

MY FATHER LIKED to teach me Chinese sayings. He didn't do this intentionally, out of any desire to educate me, but they were always bubbling up when he spoke. Inevitably, something he said would remind him of a particular proverb.

One of his favorites was a story about Kong Rong and the pears.

I had a picture book that illustrated Kong Rong—a cheerful boy with a squashed face and two rounded pigtails. He and his brothers darted around a table with a bowl of sunny green pears. Kong Rong always let his brothers have the larger pears, leaving the smaller ones for himself. This demonstrated humility and kindness, but I found it pathetic that he always yielded to someone else.

I rarely remembered my father's sayings unless he had repeated them many times. Often, I even tuned them out, because they were not useful to me, in the way that most things I learned in school were not useful. For instance, my father didn't know about the history of Jamestown, which we had spent nearly a month studying, yet it didn't seem to pose problems for him.

One day, when my father picked me up from school, he was listening to a game show on the radio. This round involved guessing the original languages of famous proverbs. Most of them ended up being from Arabic, French, or Chinese, but my father had never heard of any of them.

Then the announcer said, "To have a heart's eye."

My father muttered the words, translating them back into Chinese: 有心眼.

"This is from Chinese!" he exclaimed.

It meant to be clever—wily. Like a third eye in Buddhism, or Hinduism.

"Like the other day, in the lab," he said excitedly, gesturing out the window. "Betty was crying."

Betty was another postdoctoral fellow in his lab, but she was much younger than him. He had been a postdoctoral fellow for my entire life.

They were writing up an article on landslides. "I've been leading the project for a year," my father said. "But Betty said she won't be able to get a job next year if she doesn't get first author this time."

The show ended and he turned the volume down.

I knew that if my father didn't lead this project, he might not have his fellowship renewed. And then we would have to move.

"Why would you let her do that?" I lurched forward from the back scat, but the seat belt snapped me back.

Through the rearview mirror, I watched him smile as we turned into our neighborhood. The houses shrunk as we drove down the street.

I realized that my father might be stupid.

I thought of the boarders at home. My father had started renting out rooms to graduate students from China who were seeking a cheap place to stay. I thought of the two men, Little Wang and Samuel, who often cooked. They used so many peppercorns that the smoke scalded my eyes; the black bean sauce cast dung-like stains on the wallpaper. I thought of the woman, Cherry, and how she always left her underwear to dry on the towel rack, where the water dripped over my toothbrush. Brown stains crept along the lace trim and the sight made me want to vomit. This was how my father wanted us to live?

My father turned the volume up as we approached the house. A Beethoven sonata played, one of his happier ones.

"It's not fair!" I cried.

"Life is not fair," he said. "But that's an American saying."

When I was in college, I discovered a saying opposite from the one on the radio show: 缺心眼. *To lack a heart's eye.* It meant someone unsophisticated, simple. It meant my father.

––––––

WE LIVED IN harmony for many years.

My father continued to pick me up, even when I was in high school. It was easier for him now that I had joined the track and cross-country team. Practice lasted until the sun set, and he no longer had to go back to work after fetching me.

One afternoon, I was waiting for him at the curb in front of the school, with my teammate Ashley. It was late March. The dogwoods bloomed, lining the sidewalks with white puckered leaves and forging a canopy over the trails. By being fast, I had made friends with the other girls on the varsity team. At first I had lingered around them, to their suspicion, but Ashley had quickly pulled me into the circle. Now I was invited to their pasta dinners, held at houses with double ovens and pink marble floors and two-story foyers with Greek columns.

"You're so funny," Ashley liked to say, when I hadn't done anything funny at all. She had an easy laugh, and liked to talk about how I was different from the other Asians.

"Con-*nie*," she said. "Let's beat that Adams girl next week."

The other girls and I often rotated between the top five at races, but usually the girl from Adams High—a tall, greenishly pale girl who looked like a praying mantis—outran us all.

A honk. My father's signal. I waved goodbye to Ashley and jogged to the car.

"Good news," my father said, as I ducked in and dropped my backpack on the carpet. He had been gazing at the sunset, but turned back to greet me.

The university would renew his postdoctoral fellowship again, so we wouldn't have to move. It had been renewed twice already. But this time, he promised, he would publish something good—something groundbreaking. His supervisor had hinted that a full-time lecturer position might open soon, and he would recommend him for that.

"You really should be a professor by now," I said sulkily, "but this is great, congrats." I felt sorry for qualifying my enthusiasm.

"We should celebrate."

He drove us to the creamery, where I ordered a peach-flavored ice cream. It instantly agitated my empty, post-practice stomach. He asked for a scoop of chocolate in a cone.

"My treat," I hollered at the register. I paid with cash I had earned from babysitting.

We sat outside on metal chairs, where I told him my plan for college applications in the fall. Every week, I had been receiving brochures in the mail, glossy trifold images of leaf-spangled campuses, gleeful students, gleaming bookstacks in classrooms. They all enticed me in some way; they signaled an elsewhere I lusted after. From my research, I had chosen a slate of schools that provided scholarships—primarily on the East Coast, but some distance from our home.

My father wanted to know why I wouldn't apply to the university where he worked.

"You could live at home," he said, as we returned to the car. "You could save money."

The new boarders were three men, sloppy in the bathroom and out. I cleaned the toilet on weekends, scraping dried excrement off the back of the seat with an old toothbrush, while my father tidied the kitchen. Smells suffused the house—fish, meat, piss, sweat—and my fear of stinking at school had led me to store my clothes in knotted trash bags. In the morning, before I dressed, I held the clothes to my face and inhaled deeply, hoping I wouldn't detect anything.

"I just want to see something new," I said.

"But as a backup, at least."

I turned toward the window. The streetlights flickered past.

At home, my father jammed the key into the lock and lifted the handle before pushing it back down. The bolt often got stuck, you had to jiggle the key a certain way for it to loosen.

"I'm not like you," I said as we entered, leaving our shoes in a pile by the door and changing into slippers. "I actually want to do something with my life."

His briefcase dropped to the ground, where the buckle fell with a clang.

I thought perhaps he hadn't heard me, when he said, "What do you think I've done with my life?" He said this sharply, loudly.

"Wasted it," I said, feeling a surge of boldness from those familiar words I had heard—admonishments from teachers at school, warnings from inspirational posters. But my voice had grown soft as I delivered the line. I regretted it already.

"What?" He shuffled over, his slippers flapping against the hardwood. "Say it again."

I met his eyes. "Wasted. It." I said the two words slowly and clearly, and with each syllable I gained power; an electricity pulsed up my arms and danced in my chest.

I waited for him to respond, and the moment seemed to expand into minutes, until a ray of light slashed into the room. A car's headlights, one of the boarders pulling into the driveway.

"If I have," he said simply, finally, "it's because of you."

BEFORE I LEFT for college, I cleaned out my room. My father wanted to put it up for rent. He stated this plainly, after I made the decision to attend a school six hours from home. We were going to hold a yard sale for the things I didn't need, so I could have some spending money. Everything else would be covered by my scholarship.

All the books in the house had been moved to my room years ago, when we started accepting boarders. I tossed most of the books into crates—Shakespeare plays from school, an earth science textbook I had forgotten to return, a dozen Chinese books, with the binding on the right side, the pages scalloped with bug bites. I assumed they were my father's, from another time. Each set of books unearthed other dreary treasures from the back of the shelves: hairpins and plastic rings, sticky, melted batteries, silverfish dashing into corners.

I had finished emptying one shelf when I noticed a slip of yellowed paper on the carpet. It looked like it had fallen from one of the Chinese books. The paper was thin, almost translucent, the folded lines crisp from years pressed between pages. When I opened it, I saw that it was written in Chinese, in a neat, careful script. The handwriting wasn't my father's; I knew his scrawl, a looping, hypnotic cursive I could never decipher.

It was a poem with eight lines of text. Each line contained seven characters, and I recognized a few: *cloud, woman, wind, empty, dream, moon.* But I couldn't form a meaning.

I rushed outside, where my father was rolling the lawn mower from the garage.

"Wait!" I called from the kitchen door. The grass pricked my feet as I ran to him.

"I found this." I waved the paper.

He wiped his fingers on his shorts before taking the note.

"It's your mother's writing," he said, smiling.

"But what does it say?" Sweat fell from his eyebrows to his fingers, which he flicked away. He muttered the lines in a soft, singsong voice. It was midday, and other summer sounds crowded the air—dogs yapping, children shrieking on trampolines, lawn mowers purring from the adjoining yards.

When he finished, he said, "It's a poem by Qiu Jin."

I shook my head. I had never heard of her.

"She was a revolutionary. She fought against the Qing dynasty. And she was—how do you say it? A feminist. A talented poet. An idol for your mother."

"What's the poem about?"

"It's written for a Japanese friend," he said.

He tilted his face to the sun, as though searching it for an answer.

"It's a beautiful poem, if you can try to understand it."

I retrieved the note. He leaned toward the mower once more, and yanked the cord.

Back inside the house, I watched as my father zigzagged down the lawn with his body hunched, his arms extended straight out in front of him.

From the crates, I fished out an old Chinese-English dictionary, with a shiny red cover. Long ago, I had learned how to look up characters. But it was a complicated process that involved recognizing the radical and the number of strokes of each component of a character. I spent the afternoon writing down definitions, before struggling to construct each line.

> *Do not say that women are not heroes,*
> *As I ride eastward for thousands of miles alone.*
> *This poem's thoughts swell like a sail in the empty ocean,*
> *My dream takes me around the three islands under the*
>   *glittering moon.*
> *In sorrow I remember the copper camels already fallen,*
> *Though hard working, I am ashamed to have accomplished*
>   *nothing.*
> *So I regret and grieve over my family and country,*
> *Is it better to enjoy the spring wind as a guest?*

Some of my translations didn't make sense. For instance, what was the importance of the copper camels? And why had my mother written down this poem? She had been a scientist, like my father. What use would poetry have been to her?

I ENROLLED IN Chinese when I started my first semester. I had chosen a class for advanced students, because I could read some Chinese. But the professor taught traditional Chinese, rather than the simplified characters I had learned in Chinese School. In the library, I spent hours poring over complex pictographs. Sometimes, in the midst of one of these fevered sessions, I would remember a saying of my father's, and it would follow me through the day like music. I still carried my mother's poem with me, in my wallet, but I had given up on translating it.

The professor had a regimented approach to the language that involved hours of memorization and repetition. In class, instead of attempting to speak freely, we acted in role-playing games, with printed scripts. I began to doubt my tones, to question my pronunciations. For months, I felt as though I was learning an entirely different language, divorced from the one I spoke at home.

I HAD WANTED to pursue something useful, but in the end, I majored in Chinese. After finishing college, I worked for several years, in aimless and tiring jobs at foreign policy think tanks in Washington, D.C., until I started a doctoral degree in comparative literature, studying feminist poetics in twentieth-century China.

My father had accepted a lecturer position when I was in college, which paid more and allowed him to teach. He called often to tell stories about his students and how they lavished him with gifts—a glazed mug from the paint-your-own-pottery store, a small lamp made of a geode.

But he began to suffer while teaching classes. He became dizzy and leaned against the walls for support; his ankles became puffy as grapes. He would feel energetic and then suddenly tired. One afternoon, his body became cold, he started shivering, standing at the lectern, and a student rushed up to him to tell him he had sweated through his dress shirt.

Every weekend, he went to a Chinese restaurant called Jumbo Buffet, where he managed to charm his way into paying only a lunch fee while spending the entire day there. I joined him once. He had eaten an entire plate of shrimp for the first course, six skewers of chicken satay for the second, and was beginning the third—a tangle of crab legs.

"Don't eat so much rice," he said, eyeing my plate. "It's not worth the money."

I had been spending my days studying and writing. I no longer ran, and rarely even walked outside anymore, so my appetite had become small. Sometimes I ate only a meal a day.

"Okay," I said. "How's the teaching?"

He cracked open a leg. The shell splintered and scattered onto the table.

"You're looking pale. Don't work so hard," he said sympathetically.

"You too."

"You know," my father ventured. "When your mother died, the doctor said something to me. He said your mother had worked too hard in life." He placed the crab leg on the plate, the flesh uneaten. "She was twenty-five. Her hair had turned white. Of course, she was still beautiful. We met at the university, you know. You look like me, but you're like her. Not so straight. Not so clear-minded."

I nodded, but my breath caught in my throat, I couldn't speak.

"She had seizures." He leaned forward, rubbed his fingers vigorously on a napkin. "We didn't know the name for it. But it's something doctors look for now. She said she was fine. She said not to call the doctor. It's my fault. I should have told the doctor how many seizures she had."

He paused. "When she was pregnant with you." He looked down at his plate and back up.

My fingers were trembling. I clenched a napkin with one hand, dug my nails into my thigh with the other. The pain felt good, as though all of my being was concentrated there, and the person at the table was someone else, someone charged with answering for me.

We sat there for a long time, not speaking. I felt an unmooring in my chest, and then, for the first time, hunger. I saw at once how separate I was from my father, and as if in response to this new knowledge, a furious energy was building in my stomach, which was rising up my chest and throat, which confirmed a zeal I hadn't known in myself, some shuddering, euphoric, blasphemous thing.

My father rose to get a cup of tea, which he placed shakily on the table.

I said, "I hate you."

And then the energy was gone. We were quiet after that.

"There's a saying in Chinese," he said, after the silence.

He uttered an old idiom: 刀子嘴豆腐心. "Do you know the meaning?"

He had said this one so often that I recited the translation without thinking.

"Knife of a mouth, tofu of a heart."

"Yes," he said. "You are like that, all attitude. But inside, it's soft. I know."

He reached across the table and placed his hand awkwardly on top of mine. I didn't move. The napkin inside my hand had become damp.

Later, I would remember how his hand had been pink and hot, and how similarly our hands were shaped—small with long and slender fingers. But then I saw only his desperation, his desire to make me love him, a desire I had always known that made me not want to yield. We have only these few chances in life to surprise ourselves—to make a change, to be different from what we imagine.

But I didn't change. I removed my hand. I paid the bill, and left the restaurant.

In the car, I fumbled with my overstuffed wallet, which stored my ID and credit cards, old movie tickets, parking receipts. I dug everything out, emptying the slots onto the passenger seat. Nested within this was the note from my mother, where she had transcribed the poem by Qiu Jin. The corners were rounded and worn, but inside, her handwriting remained perfect.

I read the poem with ease. I recalled my difficulty, a decade ago, translating the "copper camels," but now I saw how obviously they represented the country the speaker had abandoned. And I realized what my mother had given up: She had moved to America for my father's job, she had relinquished her own work as a scientist, and I had lived instead of her.

I returned to school and began writing my dissertation with a kind of religious fervor.

WHEN I ANSWERED the call from the doctor's office, they had already been calling me for days.

I had turned thirty, and was finishing my doctoral degree. I was determined to win the department's dissertation award. I seldom visited home anymore. The man I was dating at the time didn't know about my background. Because my apartment was so small, we mostly stayed at his place, where he received long letters and care packages from his mother every few weeks.

"It's a miracle he's still alive," the nurse said.

They had been dialing the wrong number—my old number—and I wondered if it was the mistake of paperwork, or if I really hadn't given my father the new one.

I drove several hours to our old town in Virginia. Along the way I listened to public radio, but they didn't play any game shows like the one we had listened to years ago. Mostly, I heard the news—updates from a school shooting, an interview with a refugee about her bestselling book on escaping her home country by boat—interspersed with classical music. Beethoven, Liszt, Grieg. In my father's car, we had listened like this, barely speaking. Sometimes, when he liked a piece, I would later catch him humming the tune in the shower.

At the hospital, I found out my father had suffered from cardiac arrest after a heart attack. He had been intubated, and placed on a ventilator, but hadn't woken up.

My father shared a room with another patient, separated by a blue curtain. I drew the curtain to find my father missing from the bed. In his place was another man—small, pale, wrinkled, dressed in a striped hospital gown. My father still had traces of black hair, but this man's hair was long and white, a mop of rough plastic filaments. The blanket had been pulled up to his armpits, and one of his arms lay outside of it, pocked and dotted with violet marks. A sense of relief flooded over me. Perhaps this wasn't my father after all.

The man's wrist seemed bound by the hospital band—as if in removing it, his arm and hand would detach. On it, I caught the name: my father's. His birth date. The date he was admitted: seven days ago.

He appeared to be sleeping, and if only I shook his hand—scared him awake, as I had as a child—he would open his eyes again.

I touched his hand. His fingers were cold, but the inside of his palm was warm, almost wet. As I held his hand, his breath quickened. On the heart monitor, the graph spiked, its red line suddenly alive again, before it flattened.

THAT DAY IN the autumn storm, when my father watched me race, I missed winning by two seconds.

The girl I often competed with at our rival high school hadn't shown up, and the rain had slowed the others down. I was far ahead of everyone, turning the final curve of the course when I thought of my father standing in the rain, wearing a tan peacoat with dark buttons, an ill-fitting purchase from Goodwill, made for someone several sizes larger than him.

I thought of him and his simple life, his simple habits. In the morning, drinking a cup of milky coffee, then packing a sandwich with deli ham and Kraft cheese for lunch. In the afternoon, listening to public radio as he picked me up from practice. In the evening, boiling frozen dumplings with bok choy when we arrived home. And how he had never become anything great, how he kept applying for new positions every few years because he could never secure a tenure-track offer, he could never publish research good enough to merit it.

It was a girl from my own team who had seized the moment. I was just steps from the finish line when a slip of skin swept my arm—her arm, her elbow, her body flashing past mine, vaulting over the red webbed strip.

My father was waiting for me under a tent that had been set up for parents at the end of the course. He hovered near the edge, not speaking with the others—mostly women, mothers guarding coolers filled with Gatorade and waving homemade signs from their camping chairs, the markered letters of my teammates' names gruesomely waterstreaked.

"It's your fault!"

Those were the first words I sputtered. The pain of losing ricocheted in my stomach—the shock of placing second yet again, of failing to grasp this chance at becoming something more than ordinary for once. The anger made me cruel.

"I could have won," I cried bitterly, pushing him away as he moved forward to embrace me. It was important for me to stand apart from him, outside the tent, still under the rain.

"You're pathetic," I said, quietly, because the mothers were watching now, they held their children in their arms. I was aware, even then, of how wrong I was to say such a thing. My heart hammered in my ears from my defiance.

"What kind of parent tells their kid to *slow down*? In a *race*?"

He reached out and thumbed my arm, pinched my skin lightly, where my teammate had touched me when she sprinted past. He was smiling. He launched the yellow umbrella at the sky and coaxed me under it, throwing an arm over my shoulder, even though I was soaked and would get his clothes wet, too. He guided us toward the parking lot, where the Corolla waited. His breath was warm against my cheek as he turned to me, his voice so close it crawled under my skin.

"Remember, there's a saying in Chinese," he said.

"Knife mouth, tofu heart."

I forgave him then, as he would forgive me, for all my life.

Jessie Li was born in Hong Kong. Her writing has appeared or is forthcoming in *The New Yorker, The Atlantic, New England Review,* and *StoryQuarterly.* She is currently a Fiction Fellow at the Michener Center for Writers, where she is at work on her first book.

Editor's Note

"The Diaspora Café" is a grown-up's story: It's smart, beautifully written, and powerful. While issues of identity are central, as with so much contemporary literature, here they are engaged in subtle and often conflicting ways—there are no easy answers. No right or wrong. Over the course of the story, we see Chidi, the complex main character, grow and deepen as a result of the internal dramas that have driven her from the very beginning. I was moved, deeply, and terribly impressed with the skill and human understanding that Vince Omni displays in this marvelous piece of work. Bravo!

David Lynn, Judge
2025 Jesmyn Ward Prize in Fiction
Michigan Quarterly Review

The Diaspora Café

Vince Omni

Monday's Special: The Malcolm X Burger

A black bean and quinoa patty on a toasted gluten-free bun with tomatoes, sprouts, and spicy aioli. Served with roasted sweet potatoes.

CHIDI KNOWS FLAG MAN—SHE JUST CAN'T PLACE HIM. From where she stands in the kitchen making two specials, she watches Marshawn pour him a large dark roast, bag up an old-fashioned donut, and slide them across the glass counter. Flag Man snaps to attention and salutes Marshawn, ashy brown fingers angled against the Denver Broncos logo stitched to his orange and blue skull cap. He exits through the front door that opens onto Welton Street. Two American flags flutter from the back pocket of his tattered jeans like a mini parade. Chidi resists the urge to salute. That instinct, born from twenty years in the Army, is hard to suppress, but the black bean burgers help. Now plated, they nestle along the curve of one arm. She can feel their warmth as she watches Flag Man. Each step he takes is precise, the walk of a soldier. He huffs and a wispy cloud evaporates into the afternoon chill. Sunlight catches the chrome of bulky, tape-bound headphones clamped down over his ears. A glimmer, a blink of the eye, and he is lost amid a crowd of holiday shoppers.

The billboard over the old Ace Hardware across the street has been there since Thanksgiving, white letters popping against a light blue background. *Start your day like a superstar! Super Nova Beans and Brew! Coming in 2016!* Chidi knows this is not for sure true. Super Nova still needs to survive the city council vote next Monday. Some people in Five Points don't want the retail chain to absorb the Diaspora Café. Last weekend a customer told Chidi she shouldn't do business with Super Nova because the CEO is a member of the Illuminati. There are more pressing concerns, of course: the unfair tax incentives Super Nova is likely to receive; a spike in housing costs that follows the chain wherever it operates; and a surge in traffic that's likely to drive parking spots, those ever-elusive urban commodities, to the brink of extinction. Not that Chidi will have to worry about parking. A *yes* vote means she can sign the contract on her desk. A stroke of the pen, and just like that, she'll be rich. With more than enough money for her and Nico, her husband and junior partner, to set up the Diaspora in another part of Denver, in another city altogether, if that's what they want. They could retire, buy that RV they sometimes talk about, hit the road for a grand adventure. Or tour Africa. She's been only to Enugu, her mother's home in Nigeria, and Africa's mega cities—Lagos, Cairo, Nairobi, Dar es Salaam—call to her.

A flyer taped to the door catches Chidi's eye. It features the café's logo, a map of the Black Atlantic stamped onto a coffee cup sandwiched by the word *Diaspora* on top and *Café* on the bottom. A message printed in large bold font on the flyer announces, *The Black-Coffee-Matters Rally, 10 a.m. Saturday outside the Diaspora Café. A vote against Super Nova is a vote for Five Points! Brought to you by the Real Five Points Coalition.*

"Fucking DeAndra," Chidi mutters. She rips the flyer from the door and surveys the café for DeAndra James, head of the Real Five Points Coalition and Marshawn's older sister. All she finds are regulars: employees from the Blair-Caldwell African American Research Library across the street, undergrads with MacBooks, and a few remaining locals from when her father used to run the joint. A lot of white people. More than would have been here twenty years ago. Ten years ago. Five years ago. Two of them will be eating cold black bean burgers if she doesn't get moving. She stuffs the flyer into her apron pocket and strides over to a table where a couple sips half-finished lattes. She eases the plates down before them, collects the table marker—a tiny Kenyan flag affixed to a metal stand. She deposits the flag near the register amid dozens of others: Jamaican, Canadian, Nigerian, British, Brazilian. American. Nico, tall and light-skinned with locks that cascade down broad shoulders, stocks the shelves. She taps one of those shoulders. "Got a minute?"

He dumps squat brown packages labeled with *Direct Trade* stickers into a wicker basket and follows her into the kitchen, where Chidi asks the dishwasher to relieve Marshawn. "I need to see her now."

"What's up?" Nico asks.

Chidi hands him the flyer. The way his face relaxes when he reads, all pretense slipping away from his expression as his lips move, is one of the first things she admired about Nico when she met him six years ago while on leave in Savannah, Georgia. He sat outside a crowded café reading *Devil in a Blue Dress* and sipping a doppio, like that moment was the most important moment in his life, like he'd been born to read that book and sip espresso without a care in the world. She asked to share his table and he smiled. *Only if you tell me your name.* Three months later, they jumped the broom in front of the

Haitian Monument at Franklin Square. Nat and Olanma, Chidi's parents, and Ike, her older brother, flew down from Denver for the wedding. It had been a good day for her father. A third round of chemo for prostate cancer had gone well. His PSAs were down, and his spirits were up. He welcomed Nico to the family with a hug and clap on the back. *Call me Pops!* They got on like a house on fire. Both men were oddly handsome, artistic, charismatic. No head for business, either. Nat Creek, a.k.a. Pops, 1964 Golden Gloves champ and beloved man of the people. Never charged to rent his diner for special events. Gave food to anyone with a sad song. Nico, the perpetual artist, was ever content to create but never profit. When Chidi used to stay in his Savannah home, she found recipes sticking from books and index card containers, handmade furniture crammed to the rafters in his workshop, forgotten drafts of short stories on his desk.

"We can't afford this kind of attention," Chidi says now to Nico. "Super Nova'll walk away from this deal if they get more bad press. You saw what happened in Portland." A white Super Nova manager called the cops on two black college students in Portland. An econ major who, though he could not always afford to buy coffee, always arrived early to secure a highly sought-after table near the window, was arrested for loitering. Super Nova issued a tepid apology that did little to appease a cascade of nationwide criticism.

"Let them walk!" Nico hands the notice back to Chidi. "Pops wouldn't want this."

"We barely turned a profit this year!"

"It takes five years to see a profit. We did it in one!"

Duty, her North Star, led Chidi back to Denver when her father died two years ago. She hadn't meant to stay, had no interest in the diner. It had been too small a place to hold her and her father at the same time, so it was the Army for her. She enlisted the morning she turned eighteen and told her father about it while closing the diner that night. He hit the ceiling, said a black soldier in America was an oxymoron. *So is a business that keeps losing money.* They were the only words she could think of to wound him, to get him off her back. With him gone, she thought it might be different, but she still felt claustrophobic there, with the second mortgage, the failing HVAC system, the cracked vinyl seats she and Ike stacked on chipped Formica tables each night so they could sweep and mop the gold linoleum that curled up in the corners. And memories of Nat everywhere: in the large twenty-four-quart pots he labored over each day, in the old map of the Middle Passage their father hung behind the desk in his office. Ola, her mother, an Igbo woman who fled Nigeria in the wake of civil war, had taught her that the history of black people does not begin with slavery. Chidi never understood her father's attachment to the map, couldn't comprehend why he would want to be reminded of that history. By the time he died that had changed, as the Army had taught her a painful lesson about historical memory. Still, she wanted no part in the diner until Nico, that fount of creative energy, pitched an idea. *What if we used our savings to turn it into a café? Hang Pops's map out front and build a Black Atlantic motif around it?* Chidi fell for the possibility of making money off white interlopers. Nico called it the Diaspora Café.

Now customers pay top dollar for collard green omelets, cornmeal porridge, fried eggs and dodo. Her father's beloved chili, a steadfast staple apparently too quotidian for hipsters, does not move as well. It might sell better if they paired it with Pabst Blue Ribbon, but they're still waiting on a liquor license from the city. A few of the old regulars who haven't been pushed out to Aurora or

Green Valley Ranch still order chili to-go, carting away steaming cardboard containers in fancy paper bags bearing the café's logo. Chidi wants to scratch it from their production line, but Nico, whose hold on the menu is authoritarian, won't let her.

Marshawn sashays into the kitchen. "Hey, Nico," she says, voice sweet and gooey.

Chidi sticks the flyer in Marshawn's face. "You know about this?"

"Damn!" Marshawn rears back. "Why you comin' for me?" She takes the paper from Chidi, reads it closely, smiles.

Chidi edges forward and speaks through clenched teeth. "Did you know about this?"

"Hell naw!" Marshawn shifts her weight onto one foot. "Ain't like I'm sad about it, though." Marshawn used to sit in the dining room, hands filled with pencils or charcoal, head bent over a sketchbook. A ninth grader when Pops offered her a job at the register, she's now in her second year of art school.

Nico crosses his arms and does that thing with his eyebrow that reminds Chidi of The Rock. Marshawn examines her fingernails: blue with red streaks, like her braids. Chidi reminds herself to breathe. She's felt this way more and more of late, as if Nat is still there, his booming personality crowding the room.

"The Real Five Points Coalition," Chidi says. "That's your sister, right? DeAndra?"

"So?" Marshawn shrugs.

"So don't stand there and tell me you didn't know about this."

"See?" Marshawn says, untying her apron. "You just like these white folks around here."

The way Chidi advances on Marshawn is reflexive. The Army taught her that, too.

"Easy, babe." Nico steps between the two women.

Marshawn slides the apron over her head. "You think your name and that nappy-ass hair make you black when really you walk around here in yoga pants, ready to sell out the first chance you get." She storms out of the kitchen, around the counter and into the heart of the café. "And take that goddamn map off the wall. Don't nobody wanna see that!"

Tuesday's Special: The Miriam Makeba
Locally sourced ground lamb, minced with garlic, ginger, and shallots, and then roasted on skewers. Served with pita bread and hummus.

Chidi examines the chalkboard menu. It stands on a sidewalk trimmed in snow and ice encrusted with pollution. The sign's wording is solid, but the artwork is clumsy. A South African flag occupies too much of the menu's real estate and she's not sure about the color scheme. The rendering of Makeba is also troubling. An odd-shaped hat or scarf crowns the singer's head, which is also out of proportion and lolls to one side of her too-tiny frame. Chidi is comparing the drawing to an image of Makeba on her phone when Nico emerges from the café.

"How you like Mama Africa?" he asks.

Chidi holds out her phone for Nico to examine.

"You the one run off our artist."

"I'll hire someone."

"Why? This could all be Super Nova's problem next week." Nico is right, of course. That doesn't stop the lump forming in Chidi's throat, doesn't keep her face from burning in the afternoon chill.

Chidi nods to the menu board. "Help me get this inside. The Super Nova exec will be here soon." They each grab a side of the chalkboard and move it into the Diaspora. A rowdy knot of students spills in behind them. They wear navy blazers over white shirts and maroon ties with khaki pants or skirts. Two young men have loosened their belts so their pants sag just below their hip bones. The students shed coats and backpacks on the leather sofas and chairs arranged around coffee tables and then line up at the register, where Nico rings up orders: sandwiches, chips, hunks of bread pudding. Chidi delivers food a few minutes later to where they sit beneath her father's old map, its tattered edges flattened by glass encased in a heavy wood frame.

"The Middle Passage." The voice comes from behind Chidi.

Chidi turns and finds DeAndra standing just inside the shop. She is striking, with even brown skin that complements the camel wool coat she wears over a stylish blue suit and white sneakers. Chidi's first impulse is to run up on the woman trying to sink her deal. Doesn't matter that she's nearly six feet tall. Chidi had squared up with men in the military.

"Must be a million of us buried under that water," DeAndra says, sidling up alongside Chidi. "Maybe more."

"Definitely more."

DeAndra looks around the café, runs a hand over her close-cut, wavy hair. "My old man used to bring me here back in the day. We'd sit in a booth over there." She points to a corner with a blond college student at an ornate high-top table, scrolling on a phone. "Things are different now."

One of the first things Chidi got rid of when she and Nico took over the property were the old tables and chairs. Her father's food might have popped against Formica, but the Diaspora's menu required lacquered wood and brushed metals fashioned in Nico's workshop, the kind of baroque sophistication that put folk at ease with dropping twenty dollars on lunch.

"I don't appreciate the flyer you left on my door," Chidi says, looking up at DeAndra.

"Hey, that's you, right?" DeAndra says.

Chidi turns to face a wall of family pictures. Most of them are of Nat. A young version, with chest bare and hands bound in tape, leaning carelessly against the ropes of a boxing ring; in another, he wears a black leather jacket, with an afro stuffed under a beret, a revolutionary look he claimed got him expelled six weeks shy of high school graduation. There are photos of Nat and Ola, little Ike nestled between them, standing in front of the diner shortly after it opened in 1974, and Nat ladling chili into bowls during his annual community Thanksgiving meal. A framed newspaper article titled "Pops' Diner Celebrates 25th Year" features a photo of Nat with his elbows propped up on the ledge of the pass-through window. His smile is toothy and kind. Nothing like the smile Chidi displays in the picture DeAndra wants to know about. It was taken by Ola during Chidi's high school graduation dinner. Chidi wears her cap and gown, but the gown is unzipped, revealing an old-fashioned dress no mother had any business making her daughter wear in 1993. Chidi offers the camera a tight smile that stops well short of the eyes. Behind her, a reporter standing next to her father holds a microphone in front of his mouth. Another man aims a tripod-mounted camera at the reporter and her father. Dinner guests flank the scene. A young man had been killed by a stray bullet during a drive-by shooting the week before. His funeral was held on graduation morning. Word spread that Pops' Diner paid for the arrangements and a news team was dispatched to get the story.

"You must miss him," DeAndra says.

Chidi had not expected to miss him this much. He'd been open about cancer, how he planned to fight it, which he did for almost ten years. She thought that would be long enough for her to come to terms with his mortality, had not considered how memories live raw and close to the surface of tender places, and how those tender places hurt more, not less, as time wears on. Chidi is in the middle of this thought when the front door swings open and the exec from Super Nova, a sister clad in upscale designer fashion, walks over and shakes her hand.

"Hey, girl! Sorry I'm late. Parking is bananas! It took me twenty minutes to find a spot!" Her voice is pleasant, as it had been on the phone that morning, when she telephoned to schedule a meeting about the Real Five Points Coalition. She extends a manicured hand to DeAndra. "Portia Mitchell."

"I know who you are," DeAndra says, shaking Portia's hand. "I just always thought, when I finally met the devil, she'd be rocking Prada—not Gucci."

"You've been looking forward to meeting the devil?" Portia asks.

"I've been looking forward to whupping the devil's ass." DeAndra smiles.

"Spicy," Portia says, dialing up the wattage on her smile. "I like it." She tells Chidi she'll wait for her in the office.

"Cute," DeAndra says, when she's disappeared behind a frosted-glass door just beyond the kitchen. "I'd let her acquire me for seven figures."

"Why are you here?"

"The Diaspora is a legacy business."

"You think I don't know that?" One other café, a barbershop, and a hair stylist will be the only remaining black-owned legacy businesses in Five Points once Chidi sells the Diaspora. Three establishments. *Three!* A small number that has cost her countless hours of sleep.

"Your business helps my sister work her way through college."

"Marshawn is a trip."

"Right, she's boy crazy and addicted to IG. She also remembers when you could still buy a pig ear sandwich down the street."

"Hey, I'm from here."

"You ain't been from here for a grip." DeAndra nods to the wall of pictures. "Not the way Pops was."

"My father died in debt." The timbre of her voice, its depth and resonance, surprises her.

"Well, we'll see if Little Ms. Super Nova still wants to write you a check after the rally on Saturday. I got permits, a dope fit for the occasion, and the will of the people. Check me out on Twitter. I don't bluff, bro."

Then DeAndra is gone and Chidi wonders, why did the sister just call her *bro?*

Wednesday's Special: The Fela Kuti
Locally sourced chicken breast, soaked in Nigerian marinade and then grilled to perfection. Served with a cup of pumpkin pepper soup or plantain chips.

Otis Redding, his voice dipped in molasses, pleads for a white Christmas while Chidi bends over the sidewalk chalkboard laid out before her on a high-top table, writing Thursday's special in a spi-dery, uneven hand. She frowns before wiping the board clean with a damp towel. Nico looks up from behind the counter. Wrapping cubes of bread pudding in cellophane, he smirks. "Hard, ain't it?"

Chidi throws the towel at him. He laughs, disappears into the kitchen, humming along with Otis. She looks around to see if any-one has seen them and is relieved to find the café empty.

A notification sounds on Chidi's phone: a message from Portia. *Great talk yesterday. Any word on the rally? There's a 10 percent bump in your bottom line if you can defuse that situation.* Chidi replies, *Still working on it.* A ten percent *bump*, by itself, would be enough to keep the Diaspora humming for the foreseeable future in a differ-ent location. Maybe someplace like Northfield, which is no longer a field, but a district filled with condos, trendy shops, eateries, and big-name department stores. Perfect place for a café.

Chidi's phone pings again. Twitter. More irate comments choke the café's feed.

Make Five Points Black Again!!!

Pops brought us the best chili in the Mile High and an annual Thanksgiving celebration. Chidi brought us some boogee-ass coffee and gluten-free bread. Far as I'm concerned, Super Nova can have the place. It ain't for us no more.

Chidi Creek is a sellout! #isaidwhatisaid

Chidi calls up DeAndra's feed for the fifth time that day. DeAndra's post about the Black-Coffee-Matters Rally is now up to 7,954 likes. Chidi's no stranger to social media melee. A small but very vocal cadre of activists tried to drag her during the rebrand. That campaign never gained much traction because people gave her the benefit of the doubt as Pops's daughter. But this? She slams her phone onto the table, closes her eyes, and sucks in a deep breath. When she opens them again, her mother and Ike stand before her, swathed in layers of wool and all manner of winter garments.

Chidi starts, holding a hand to her chest.

"This is why I don't like cell phones," Ola says. "They make you stupid."

"She's not stupid," Ike says. "Just tired from being dragged on Twitter." His tone suggests that he believes this treatment to be justified.

"Yes, I see it now. The Twitter must be very heavy if she is unable to even stand and greet her mother."

Chidi rises from her chair. "Hello, Mother." She kisses Ola on the cheek and straightens the knit hat on her head. "How are you?"

"We are going to see the lights on Sixteenth Street," Ola says.

Ike points to the ceiling. The glimmer in his eye reminds Chidi of their father. "Papa used to love this song."

Ola's smile cuts dimples in her smooth dark skin. "Otis."

Ike nods. "He always called singers by one name." They list the greats: Marvin, Aretha, Stevie, Patty, Luther, Millie, Michael, Whitney, Prince, Chaka.

Ike adds, "He always said the Temptations got him through the Blizzard of '82."

Ola shakes her head. "Three days stranded in this place? Can you imagine?"

Christmas Eve, 1982, Chidi had not wanted her father to go to work. At home, away from the diner, away from the public, he was a different man. He would play thumb war with her, hold up his palms and let her punch them as hard as she could, offer her his feet to stand on while they danced to Fela or the Jacksons. Mom tried to allay her fears with jollof rice and pepper chicken. In the end, it was Ike who succeeded in distracting her from worrying about their father being trapped at the diner. When the blizzard finally stopped and sunlight dazzled across slick banks of snow, Ike flung his bundled adolescent form from a second-story window out onto three-foot dunes of deep, crisp white. It took him two minutes to wade through the snow to the garage, and longer than that to clear away enough snow to open the garage's back door. Once inside, he raced upstairs and leapt again out onto frosty bluffs—and Chidi followed him. The cold seared her lungs, snot slid along the ridge of her upper lip, but she laughed, imagining how her father would want this joy for her.

Chidi watches her mother stare at the wall of family photos, her expression revealing that she, too, has been transported to another time. Ola removes a picture of herself, Nat, and Ike standing in front of the diner back in '74. She smiles down at the image, opens her purse, as if to slip the framed photo inside its ample folds, then decides to hang it back on the wall. This open longing is too much for Chidi, who looks away and wipes at the corners of her eyes.

"Ike! Mama Ola!" Coming out from the kitchen and around the counter, Nico hugs them both, and Chidi is a bit jealous. Nico's hugs are like all the best things—egusi and fufu, the perfect pair of jeans, a rerun of *Bad Boys* on late-night television—all rolled into one. An embrace of the soul.

Nico invites Ola and Ike to sit at the counter for fresh sweet potato scones. Chidi is about to lock the door when she notices a group of people across the street in front of the Blair-Caldwell Library. A kid sitting on a white bucket drums a complex rat-a-tat-tat on another white bucket in front of her. Her ears are covered by a thick headband, and her hair is cut into a tall high-top fade that sways slightly each time she nods to the beat. Chidi's seen this kid drum before, at the Safeway on Clarkson and at the Glenarm, but not in front of the library. Maybe her being here is a kind of warm-up to DeAndra's rally. Chidi is across the street before she realizes what she's doing. The cold is sharp. It burns her nostrils and takes her breath away. When she can breathe again, her breath hangs thick and cloudy before her eyes. She works her way into the growing crowd, looking for DeAndra. The cold is less intense there, where people rock back and forth to the beat. She slips between two larger bodies, and then, just like that, she has a clear view of the show. There, in the middle of the circle, is Flag Man.

How does she know this man with the orange and blue Broncos skully pulled nearly over his eyes? Still, his movement is fluid, melding seamlessly with the drum. He dougies, body shifting from left to right, feet shuffling in time with the beat, hands working in a way that makes the dance look more complex than it is. The cadence changes up, and Flag Man widens his stance. He locks his arms behind the shoulders of an imaginary person and grinds the air obscenely. A series of pelvic thrusts, a rhythmic swinging of hips. He bends down low and twerks before sweeping his torso up from the ground, arms outstretched like Michael Jackson. His spin is swift and furious, and when it is done, he's all B-boy: popping and locking, rocking, windmilling. He punctuates his solo with a one-handed handstand, and the crowd explodes. Flag Man then withdraws the American flags from his back pocket and plants them in a bank of dirty snow and ice. Snapping to attention, he salutes the flags in time with the beat.

Shuffle-shuffle, slide, salute. Shuffle-shuffle, slide, salute.

Chidi isn't sure what to make of this patriotic line dance, but the crowd loves it.

Go, Stanley! Go, Stanley! Go, Stanley!

Chidi's mind whirs and clicks. *Stanley Fisher!*

The audience throws money into a hat on the sidewalk until the police show up and tell everyone to disperse. Shouts and curses erupt from the crowd. Police cuff one vocal young man and make him sit in slush. Bystanders watch from behind smartphones. Chidi sees the drummer retrieve a few crumpled bills from the hat and press them into Stanley's hand. He waves her off, fastens that set of battered headphones over his ears, and retreats up Welton Street.

Thursday's Special: The Harriet Tubman
Red beans, onions, carrots, and peppers, stewed with smoked turkey. Served with a cornbread muffin.

Chidi is in the middle of inventory when Stanley walks into the café midmorning. Two library employees sit at a table by the window, where they chat over lattes and sweet potato scones. Across the room, a man reads the Qur'an and scribbles notes into a journal.

"Hey, Stanley." Chidi smiles as she approaches the register. "I saw you cuttin' up last night. I haven't seen you move like that since high school."

"I know you?"

"Chidi," she says. Then, when he does not remember: "We went to Jackson High together. You choreographed a routine to Out-Kast. 'Crumblin' Erb.' Shut the whole joint down!"

Stanley nods. "Marshawn here?"

Chidi rearranges her face into a neutral expression. "She doesn't work here anymore."

He digs into his pocket, pulls out a ten-dollar bill, and places it on the counter.

"Coffee?"

"No." He paces in front of the counter, headphone cord trailing behind him. "No, no, no!"

Customers crane necks toward the commotion.

Nico emerges from the kitchen, apron dusted with flour.

Chidi doesn't even flinch.

"Everything alright out here?" Nico joins Chidi at the counter, then crosses his large, muscled arms.

"We're good." Chidi keeps her eyes on Stanley. "Right, Stanley?" She searches his face until their eyes connect. "We're good?" Stanley looks at Nico as if just realizing the man is there.

"Nah," Nico says, untying his apron.

Chidi lays a hand on his shoulder. "I got this." Nico might look like The Rock but that's about as far as that comparison goes. Inside, he is softer than whatever confection he's concocting in the kitchen. Stanley, on the other hand, is a trained soldier. She is sure of it.

Nico hesitates, then retreats to the kitchen.

Chidi waits for the sound of the mixer to resume before speaking again. "What's the money for, Stanley?"

"Marshawn." He sets his headphones on the counter and removes the Broncos hat, revealing a forest of black woolly hair twisted into half-formed locks. Some sections are dry and matted. "She bought me breakfast the other day. I promised to hit her up when my money from the VA come in." He taps the bill on the counter.

"I can help."

"Just gimmie her address."

"I can send it to her. If I drop it in the mail today, she should have it by Christmas."

"How I know I can trust you?"

"Again, we went to the same school, sat together in science. We made fun of Mr. Kim because he was cockeyed and would point at us while looking at the other side of the room." His expression remains flat.

She straightens up and swings her arm into a taut salute, the movement still exact, as if she'd never stopped doing it. "Lieutenant Chidiogo Creek, Company A, 2nd Battalion, 3rd Infantry Division, United States Army."

"Iraq?"

"Two tours."

Stanley snaps to attention and returns the salute. "At ease, soldier." Stanley relaxes.

"Is the VA helping with that PTSD?"

He shakes his head and casts his eyes toward the array of baked goods arranged on a tray under glass. "I demobbed in Fort Liberty a few years back."

"North Carolina?"

Stanley nods. "Had me at some inpatient joint in Durham for a while. Antidepressants and whatnot. Didn't feel right, ya know?" His fingers play across the glass. "Like some kinda watered-down version of me. Drifted for a while. Made it back home about six months ago."

"So, now you just dance up and down Welton Street?"

"Gets down for them that can't get up," Stanley says.

"And that's how you want to spend your life?"

"I owe it to them. It's what they need."

"The dead?" Chidi scrunched up her face. "What do they need?"

"To be remembered, Lieutenant."

Silence falls between them. It feels right, like communion or rain or leaping from a second-story window onto a frosty plane of snow. When the moment passes, she says, "I refused to salute one morning during flag presentation. That man who murdered Trayvon had just got off, and . . ." She waves a hand. "I was arrested, court-martialed, dishonorably discharged. Had a good lawyer, so I kept my benefits and most of my pension, which I sank into this business, my daddy's business. Now, I'm going to sell it for an obscene amount of money. Honestly, I don't know what scares me most—selling it or letting it fail."

Stanley doesn't say a word, just stands there scrutinizing baked goods.

"Stanley?"

"I owe Marshawn seven dollars for that breakfast," he says, squatting down in front of the glass display now. His index finger taps the space before a row of cake donuts, their tops glossy with thick glaze. "I got enough change left for one of these old-fashioneds?" A blink. A breath. A nod.

"Cool." He pops up and claps his hands together.

Chidi bags a donut, deposits the ten into the register, and withdraws a five and two singles. She makes a show of depositing the bills into an envelope and writing Marshawn's name on it. Stanley stuffs the donut into his coat pocket, returns the skully to his head, and exits the café without his headphones. Chidi rushes to the door with them, but Stanley has already disappeared into the crowd. She wraps the long cord around the headphones. When she looks up, she is face-to-face with pictures of her father. Her mind flashes back to an evening long ago. Her father on his knees in the living room, hands held out like targets. Six years old, she stands in front of him, firing jabs and right crosses into his open palms until she stops, suddenly serious.

"Ike says I hit like a girl."

"You hit like a Creek," her father says, pulling his hands up into boxing position. "You know how a Creek hits, right?"

"Hard." Chidi's voice is tentative.

"You asking?" Nat says, throwing a soft jab wide of her head. "Or telling?"

Chidi resumes sparring, her little fists striking her father's open palms.

"That all you got?"

She punches harder, tightening her fists at the point of contact, then snapping back the way he'd shown her. Each blow she lands produces a satisfying smack against his hands. She continues this onslaught until she is out of breath, until her father shakes his hands to chase away the pain and scoops her up over his shoulder and carries her into the kitchen for dinner.

Friday's Special: The Huey Newton and Bobby Seale

Southern-fried chicken over a buttermilk waffle. Served with butter and habanero-infused maple syrup.

The breakfast crowd has died down inside the café, but Welton Street still hums with life. Traffic, unrelenting even amid a fresh coat of snow, streams north toward Downing Street. A group of tourists, armored with the latest in high-tech outdoor fashion, pose for a picture in front of the Blair-Caldwell. The light-rail grinds to a stop at the corner, dislodging more tourists, downtown professionals playing hooky from work, and holiday shoppers. Chidi and Marshawn, shoulder to shoulder outside the Diaspora, fix their attention on the chalkboard menu.

"Is that a waffle or a frisbee?" Marshawn tilts her head from one side to the other.

"I think it's supposed to be the top of Bobby's beret."

Marshawn leans in for a closer look. "Why does that chicken leg look like a fist?"

"Power to the people?" Chidi executes a tentative Black Power salute.

"Covered with syrup?"

A shrug, a laugh. "I know, right!"

Marshawn swings her braids around. "This why you got me out of bed this morning? To fix your menu board?"

"Look, I was legit out of pocket Monday. And, as you can see," Chidi says, gesturing toward the menu, "we need you."

Marshawn eyes a braid whose tip somehow escaped the flame that melted the other frayed tips into hard knots.

"I'm not selling to Super Nova."

Surprise flashes across Marshawn's face. "For real?" Chidi hands Marshawn an envelope.

Marshawn opens it, removes a five-dollar bill and two singles. She smiles. "Stanley?" Chidi nods.

Marshawn pulls out a pay stub next. "And you're paying me for the whole week?"

"Plus a holiday bonus. No matter what you decide."

That night Chidi wheels a cart across Welton Street to the library. Nico is with her. So are Ola and Ike. Another crowd has formed to listen to the young woman drum. The cart is loaded with carafes of hot coffee, platters of cookies, cream, sugar, and paper cups and napkins. Chidi parks the cart alongside the crowd, fills a cup with coffee, and offers it to an older woman in a blond wig and a red wool coat. The woman nods thank you and cradles the cup in her naked hands. Chidi pours more coffee while Ola lines up cups of the steaming brew. Nico and Ike duck in and out of the crowd, handing out treats. When Chidi glimpses DeAndra at the edge of the fray, she cuts short her chat with a poet who wants to host an open-mic night at the Diaspora.

"DeAndra." Chidi holds out a cup of coffee. "No sugar, no cream."

"How'd you know?"

"Educated guess." She smiles.

"Heard the deal with Super Nova is dead."

"Marshawn talks too much." Chidi's tone is light, playful even. "What, change your mind already?"

"Hey, I don't bluff, bro." Chidi winks.

A cheer erupts and Chidi sees Stanley in the middle of the circle. He whips, then hits a wild Nae Nae replete with a stanky leg and a couple of well-placed dabs, his head tucked into the crook of one arm while the other arm stretches out at an obtuse angle. He switches over to B-boy mode next, toprocks like it's going out of style. He sticks each pose hard, then picks the beat back up with ease. He dips and pivots, leans down low and slaps the ground, spins up into position, and starts rocking again. Chidi marvels at his stamina, his sheer athleticism. She's not the only one. People who danced just a few minutes earlier now stand still, their hands clasped around smartphones that record Stanley's every move.

More phones come out when he deposits his pocket-sized American flags into a nearby mound of snow. The day's accumulation has left it a fresh blanket of white that complements the red and blue of the flags. Stanley gets busy.

Shuffle-shuffle, slide, salute. Shuffle-shuffle, slide, salute.

Each shuffle is precise. Each slide reminiscent of James Brown. Each salute snaps the air like a TV sound effect.

Go, Stanley! Go, Stanley! Go, Stanley!

The whoop-whoop of the siren is different tonight. Its peal, eerie and sinister, splits the air. Red and blue lights fill the dark with gloom. The cruiser jumps the curb and police jump out on booted feet. "Disperse!" a voice calls into the crowd through a PA system. But no one moves. They are all transfixed by Stanley's tribute.

Shuffle-shuffle, slide, salute. Shuffle-shuffle, slide, salute.

He's huffing now, cheeks puffing out between slides. Sweat soaks through his skully, darkening the orange part. Still, he persists. Even when the police restrain the kid on the bucket to stop her drumming. Even when they stand in his path, Stanley doesn't stop. They tase him, subdue him, pour him into the back of a police cruiser. The crowd jeers. Someone throws a snowball at one officer, prompting him to call for backup. In the back of the cruiser, Stanley rights himself, presses his face against the window.

Shuffle-shuffle, slide, salute. Shuffle-shuffle, slide, salute.

Chidi takes up the spot near the flags in the snow, where Stanley danced only minutes earlier. Her first movements are stiff and awkward. It takes her a few tries to pick up the rhythm of the slide, shuffle her feet at the right time, slide across the ground with ease and style. The salute requires no practice. It is sharp and crisp. Round and round she goes, feet in a trance. The sound of the drum surprises her. She looks up the sidewalk and finds the kid with the high-top fade once again in front of her bucket, sticks pounding out a complex rhythm.

Shuffle-shuffle, slide, salute. Shuffle-shuffle, slide, salute.

The lingering crowd gathers around her, rocks to the beat.

Go, Chidi! Go, Chidi! Go, Chidi!

By the time the police return to the circle, five more people, including Ike, have fallen in alongside Chidi. Their movements are defined and in sync, as if they've rehearsed the dance. One by one, more people join the slide. The protest continues in this fashion until there are more people dancing than not. Until Nico places himself between Chidi and the police and is forced face down in the snow, hands cuffed behind his back. Until police wrangle Chidi and other sliders into the back of a police wagon.

Vince Omni is a visiting English instructor at Lake Forest College in Illinois and a McKnight Doctoral Fellow in English at Florida State University. He holds an MFA from the University of Kansas. His work earned the 2024 Jesmyn Ward Prize in Fiction and the CRAFT 2025 Novelette Print Prize. His short story "Mine Own" will appear in *Virgin Islands Noir* (Akashic Books) in 2026.

Editor's Note

"Little Women" centers on two sisters moving into adulthood in a religious family, and their changing relationship when one gets engaged. Over the years, I've come to admire stories that are doing heavy work with a light touch. Quiet and thoughtful, they aren't working hard for our attention, and they move delicately through big questions and big emotions. Megan Tennant's "Little Women" is the perfect example of this. It was also a perfect fit for *The Common*, since we focus on work with a real sense of place. The story is set in South Africa, primarily on the Wild Coast, where white tourists enjoy roughing it in coastal terrain populated for generations by the Xhosa people. The ghost of apartheid hangs like a mist over this setting, as do questions of spirituality, intimacy, and belonging. It's all so perfectly pitched, I still can't quite believe it's a debut.

Emily Everett, Managing Editor
The Common

Little Women

Megan Tennant

1.

IN DECEMBER, ONE OF THOSE NOTHING AFTERNOONS after Christmas, my younger sister, Ruth, returns to the holiday house, where I am bored with extended family on the stoep. The guests get up, ready to greet them, while my dad finds chairs for her and David. But she pauses with a funny look on her face, as if she's remembered a dream or eaten something sweet, and says she's engaged. Now everyone rises, and I make my own lips follow in a smile. David is bashful behind her, accepting hugs and handshakes. I'd like to ask him why he didn't tell me he was going to propose, ask my parents if they knew. Of course they knew.

My aunt takes pictures of our family—David now snug among us, Ruth with her hand splayed. There are pictures of us on this stoep as children, holding the Easter eggs we found in the Wild Coast overgrowth of what one might call a garden below. It's thoughtful of David to propose in Mbotyi, somewhere on those shaggy hills overlooking the sea, and for them to return to celebrate in the house that has been ours for three generations. While it was still part of the old Transkei, my great-grandfather bought the land from a chief for three bottles of sherry—a story my family used to share freely, even humorously. But it's been gradually left out of our repertoire, like an ivory heirloom we pretend not to own.

Besides the engagement, we'll remember this holiday as the

one with the bedbugs. They seem to live only in the bed where Ruth and I sleep, but somehow they haven't touched her. As we smile at the camera, I joke that I'll be the sister in the pictures with bites on her face. My older brother, Rory, laughs and hits me in the side, then hugs me.

I'll also remember this holiday as the one when I work on a tan, as responsibly as I can. After three years away, I am trying to re-bond with my country. I read books by local authors, wait for low tide to run the beach back and forth, but feel restless amid my surroundings—the sounds of speedboats through the mangroves, the screams of city children in the waves. Also, I don't know what I'll be doing come January—what paying job my new "meaningful" master's might get me, what city that job would take me to, the person I could or could not meet there. Ruth's news disorients me further.

In the evening, after the aunts and uncles and cousins have left, we pick at turkey leftovers in the kitchen. Before we peel off to bed, Ruth suggests we close with a prayer. We all bow our heads, the buzz of the fluorescent light and grasshoppers growing louder in the silence. I hear the tones of my dad—earnest, grateful—and I feel my head become heavy, my closed eyes twitching. Since I was young, following the prayers of others has made me feel sleepy, almost drunk.

2.

It was in a furniture store in Durban Central. We were buying a bunk bed for me and Ruth and were passing the double beds piled with duvets and cushions on show. I asked my mom whether anyone could share a bed when they grew up.

"Only if they're married," she'd said.

"Not even a man and a woman who are friends?"

She looked thoughtful for a moment, then said, "No, only a husband and wife sleep in the same bed."

3.

In the house in Mbotyi, Ruth and I have always slept in the second bedroom. It has only a double bed, which we pretend to resent sharing. When we were younger, during blackouts, we'd carry our candles to our night tables, pretending we were Meg and Jo in *Little Women*, who shared a bed, too.

This holiday, David's been given a mattress to sleep on in my grandfather's old study next door. Around bedtime each night he and Ruth have gone in, the light on and door ajar. I hear them while I read, talking in warm breaths. When she finally comes to bed, she gets in solemnly, as if entrusted with some important duty.

Tonight she stays with David longer. There's more silence between them, filled by the sound of clothing scratching against a blanket. I close my book early, fall asleep before she returns.

4.

January comes—a funny month in the Southern Hemisphere. In London, the Christmas lights will have come down and there'll be a good stretch of cold to help people out of the holiday slump. But back in Durban, everyone tries to refind their routines as the temperatures climb further into summer.

Ruth enters the year with the knowledge that she now has a partner forever, and I search for jobs from my parents' house. Family friends welcome me back from my studies, then ask about the wedding plans. I appear gracious, excited, but conscious of my appearance in a way I never used to be—my hair, my skin, my weight. On one visit my aunt asks if they've picked a date. It makes me remember a friend's engagement party from years ago, how her sister had gone around handing out save-the-date magnets. I'd felt sorry for her, the single older one, but at least she was still very pretty. Now I realize that she couldn't have been older than twenty-four, younger than I am now.

My family and I were only spectators at weddings until my brother, Rory, got married two years ago. Then, we sat at the main table above the other guests, and I felt like a cast member in a show we were putting on for the first time. The music stopped at midnight, and the MC directed everyone to send off the couple. Ruth and I found ourselves at the end of the tunnel we all made. As Rory and his wife ran under our arms and into the car, we watched after them, sharing the weight of a story that had ended. It was hard knowing that our family car or a Christmas morning could no longer contain just the five of us. But the pain felt right—like growing pains, an expansion.

The pain feels different this time. I think about how, each morning in Mbotyi, Ruth took a camping chair to a far corner of the stoep. She stared out beyond her open Bible and had what I assume were long chats with God. She still managed to escape dish duty and sulked when she was losing in Monopoly, things I'd expect her to grow out of before finding herself married. But maybe everything seems conquerable through a promise from God, perhaps delivered to David in a moment in church when he realized he wanted all of Ruth.

They've started attending marriage preparation classes. The

girls in Ruth's house-share have created a vision board for her in their kitchen, both as a sort of planner for the wedding and for the readying of her soul. There are cutouts of things from bridal magazines and lines from worship songs with words like "surrender" and "blessed." I eye out the updates on my visits, wondering if I dare make fun of them to Ruth—the choice of flowy font, a picture of a woman with open palms. It's on one of these visits that Ruth tells me she's invited Grace to be a third bridesmaid, in addition to me and her best friend, Crystal. "Why?" I ask. Grace is five years older than Ruth, two years older than me. "Are you that close?"

"I think Grace would be a good idea as a sort of mentor person," she says, "being married."

I picture Grace, two rows ahead of me in church, her husband's hand resting on her back. When everyone shakes hands at the Sign of Peace, they usually kiss. Faithful enough to be rewarded with lifetime love, Grace is an obvious choice.

5.

By February, I'm still on the job search. My studies now seem vague and impractical when I scan the requirements on the listings. And the jobs that I might have the skills for—copywriting, market research—don't seem to serve any greater good. I get restless, download a dating app. I set a generous radius and match with Paul from Pietermaritzburg.

He makes the effort to drive into Durban on the first date. We get a coffee, settle on a bench in Mitchell Park. I tell him about my time in London and play down the second master's I've just completed, all the while relishing his impressed nods. After a ski season in the States, he's found himself in the backwaters of

KwaZulu-Natal, and we strike up a snobbish affinity—that travel-
ing has made us more broad-thinking and restless than our peers,
while carefully acknowledging the aspects of our race and class
that have allowed us to feel these things.

"He's going to cook dinner for me," I tell Ruth, when she asks
how the date went.

"Where, in Pietermaritzburg?" she asks. "Should you be trav-
eling home so late?"

I shrug, let her read into my silence. I'll tell my parents that I'm
sleeping at a friend's. Ruth's brow quivers and I know she is wondering whether to question my plan. I am snatching something
from her, creating my own shortcuts.

6.

The bridesmaids agree to share a gift for the hen party. We decide
on matching nightgowns for the couple.

"And I'll add some practical things," says Grace.

I buy the gowns from a high-end chain that Ruth and I usually
only browse on Instagram. As I watch the shop attendant wrapping
them in tissue paper, I remember the games Ruth would make me
play when we were young, if I was feeling kind.

Ruth wants the hen party, like the wedding, at our house in
Mbotyi. Grace and Crystal seem reluctant; I am ambivalent—
impressed that Ruth is making her friends brave the five-hour
drive, the dirt roads alone, but less thrilled by the idea of a group of
white girls wandering the place in showy sashes and flower wreaths.

We arrive in May, a week before the wedding. Ruth and I take
the second bedroom as always, and let Grace and Crystal share the
master bedroom. The others set up Christmas beds in the lounge.

We walk to the beach. The sun is behind banks of consistent gray clouds. I'm the only one swimming; the rest walk the bay in little groups. Since being home, I've taken every opportunity to swim in the sea, to find meaning in the natural beauty here, pretending it's neutral, pure.

The next day, we gather on the stoep with champagne and snacks. Despite my advising her that no one really cares to sit and watch, Ruth unwraps her gifts. She gasps at the nightgowns. While she holds hers up, I spy some pharmacy items nestled in the paper.

"You can open those later," Grace says. "Some handy things for the honeymoon."

When the others get up to refill their plates, my eyes drift to the pile of new lingerie among the other gifts. More underwear than I could dream of. I push away the thought of Ruth waking up, walking around in her nightgown, somehow older, somehow older than me.

In the evening we walk to the restaurant at the backpackers' hostel—past the sparsely stocked spaza shop, a group of local children calling us for sweets, a cow pulling at the roadside grass. My grandfather used to say that this place, like most of the former Transkei, attracts a certain kind of person. He obviously didn't mean the Xhosa people who lived here, but the visitors with free spirits who craved remote places. He also meant they were white and owned four-by-fours. During apartheid, the government and developers left this area alone, disinterested in its stubborn terrain. Most would say that not much has changed—the roads turn to mud when the rain comes, the land is still resistant. The region seems ringed by a blessing or curse.

We reach the backpackers' to find it surprisingly full. A group of hikers are checking in at the reception, their calves flecked with mud, their unclipped backpacks piled on an old couch by the counter. In the restaurant area, there's a table outside that might have space. I ask the guy at the edge of it, who raises his eyes dreamily from the rolling paper in his fingers. When we're seated, I look around at the other guests. Most of them are barefoot, a little unraveled round the edges, especially compared to our own party, which has arrived in closed shoes and makeup. A staff member comes to ask what we want to drink. We order the same quarts of beer that the people next to us are drinking, an unvoiced pact to try to fit in.

It's sometime after supper when I see the girl in white. She's at the campfire, kneeling oddly and talking to the other people in the way a salesperson would—her shoulders open, a cock to her head. Crystal sees me looking at her.

"She spoke to me earlier," she whispers. "She says she's training to be a sangoma."

There's a rope around the girl's waist. Her dress looks like it's made from a stiff cotton, cut just above the knee, making the outfit look chic, almost.

"I didn't know there could be white sangomas," I say.

"Her mom told me it can happen to anyone—the ancestors call you," Crystal says. "She's visiting from Cape Town."

Crystal turns her head to a group of middle-aged people eating supper. The two women sip white wine, the man has a whiskey.

"The brown-haired one."

The woman is tanned, wears a knit jersey and tennis shoes. She reminds me of the mothers of girls I knew at school, who never worked and drove them to extracurricular activities in their SUVs.

"Her daughter was having all these dreams and headaches until they figured out she was being called."

"To do what?" I ask, impatient with Crystal's wide eyes, her breathy tone.

"To be a healer. She's living in a hut somewhere with a real sangoma while she trains. Her mom said the headaches stopped—just like that. As soon as she agreed to come here."

I almost roll my eyes. I can imagine the woman relaying this to her tennis friends in Cape Town, who are fascinated with her daughter's surprising vocation. A white person assured by the higher powers that she belongs in this country, has a role to play. Proof, by extension, that they all must, too.

I look back toward the campfire. The girl is around Ruth's age. Her eyes wear the same mesmerized look of people on drugs at festivals, except she is engaged in what looks like a very lucid explanation of her calling.

"She's been going round to all the tables," Crystal says. "Sometimes she gives people things from that brown pouch round her waist—herbs or something."

I turn back to our own table, hoping she doesn't approach me. If she's supposed to be in training, what is she doing fraternizing among all the tourists at the backpackers', with its burger special and cheap beer? I don't believe that her calling is real, that she really understands the sacrifices she'd need to make. Although, maybe this is the point of faith.

7.

God has never made me convicted about something, sure of the path before me. Instead, I've felt like a bystander that witnesses the faith of others. I wonder if they pray more, somehow believe better. And that this rewards them with a clear vocation, prophetic dreams, strong intentions.

Paul and I have continued to see each other, but the distance between Durban and Pietermaritzburg is an excuse for not making our visits more regular. We like each other, which comes from a shared understanding of going about the world: with tolerance, independence, a tendency not to lose ourselves in things. Halfway through our meetups, he usually takes my hand and starts to stroke it. I know it's more for the touch of someone than any particular affection for me.

Sometimes this has led to me staying over at his. Sometimes at the dinner table back home, when my family starts to discuss the wedding or bow their heads in prayer, I take my thoughts to my nights with Paul—the brand-new feeling of a stranger's bed.

8.

At her makeup trial, the beautician gave Ruth a tip: that when she does Ruth's face on the day, they should be alone and silent. It will be the only time Ruth will have to herself.

I doubt Ruth will take the advice—she'd want me for company at least. But when the day arrives, one of the last hot days in Mbotyi, she closes the door of our bedroom to be alone. The photographer is given access; I see evidence from the pictures after. There's a typical shot in black and white: Ruth's lashes lifting to be painted, her pupils far away. In another picture, I am reminded how young she is, perhaps by how the hairpiece makes her look like a princess.

She was stressed, she tells me later, once we're allowed into the room to help her dress. The feeling is bittersweet, less certain than she anticipated. Her head on my mom's lap the night before, she'd wondered what would change—if she could still claim her youngest place in the family, falter into dodging the dishes, her sulks. A part of me wants to console her, but another objects to the role she wants to keep. Ruth, who'll share a bed with her husband, who'll leave me to sleep in the second bedroom alone.

We've created an aisle that starts at the top of the stoep, where the bridal party will descend to the guests in the garden, and David at its edge.

I'm the final bridesmaid to make my way down. I'm reminded of school prize-giving, a careful walk to collect my award. I smile for the entire ceremony, so no picture can show anything other than joy.

When it's over, Ruth is given to the guests. The only moment we share is just before her speech, as she leans in close to me at the table and pleads for an anxiety pill she left in our bedroom. I linger for a second, reminded that she still needs me, before I jump up.

She leaves just before midnight. The dance floor fizzles shortly after, exhausted by the joy of the sober crowd.

9.

I'm woken by the cicadas early in the morning, the bedroom fully light and hot. My head and legs feel heavy, as if I really have had a long night of drinking and the alcohol is sitting in my veins. I find myself in thoughts of half sleeping, allowing them to escape from me, to become their own entities, entire scenes. The sangoma-in-training approaches my table at the backpackers' and begins to defend her calling. How the spirits have no skin color, how all she could do was surrender. I am jealous, and then drowsy, wishing she would stop talking.

It's 8:45 when I wake up again. I lie in the center of the bed, let my limbs stretch to each side. I think of what I'd like to do once we've cleaned up. I feel the expectation of a holiday, the restlessness that has followed me since I returned home. Maybe I should run to the beach and have a swim. And I wonder if the sangoma wasn't trying to convince me about anything but rather asking what I'm still doing here. Then I think about Paul, that I haven't replied to the message he sent two days ago.

The night before the wedding, as Ruth and I lay in this bed, she asked about him. She was trying to sound casual, to hide her confusion about the relationship's lack of momentum. Ruth believes in the importance of guarding one's heart, hers having never been broken. As we lay there, I knew any answer I gave wouldn't make sense to her. I know she thinks I'm involving myself with someone who has no real intentions. But I don't know if I have intentions either—for him, for returning here, returning home. If only that's what faith could be—unfolding, unsure. I turned away and said good night. I waited for her breathing to deepen in the dark.

Megan Tennant is a writer and instructional designer based in Cape Town, South Africa. Her poetry has appeared in various South African literary journals. She holds master's degrees in creative writing from the University of Cape Town and London studies from Queen Mary University of London.

Editor's Note

Zhenglong Yang's cinematic "Ride Me Up to Heaven" offers its reader a world of the night—a fruit stand, a polluted river in winter, a chain bridge, a sex toy shop—which is as much an integration of the characters' inner lives as it is a demonstration of the facts. Place deepens the story's dreamlike landscape, a world of secrets, desire, and erotic trouble. But it doesn't rest on vibe alone. It's propelled by a daring narrative of a fractured marriage told through the dual perspectives of a husband and wife at a crossroads. Their relationship unfolds with such panache, wit, and heartbreak that it's easy to overlook how difficult it is to pull off such a story—what boldness! By the end, we're left with a confession uncertain and powerful: an eruption of tenderness that feels like both an ending and a beginning.

Paul Lisicky, Editor
StoryQuarterly

Ride Me Up to Heaven

Zhenglong Yang

MA DAN'S HUSBAND WAS WORKING THE NIGHT SHIFT that Friday night and wouldn't come home until Sunday morning. The seven o'clock news was over. She had called earlier. He didn't answer. Twenty minutes later, he called back. The sound of playing cards was in the background. There were other occasions when a man addressed her husband as darling and the line went dead suddenly. Her husband was not the type of man who was good at hiding things, and she was not the type of wife who was good at making a fuss, and saw no reason to.

When the street became quiet and she had nothing to do, she went to bed. Winter was over, but the sheets remained cold. The street was muffled by April rain and warmth, but they were kept out of doors. Lying in bed, she gazed at the jelled dildo for a while, pushed it into her body, the foam clucking; she let out a moan. She knew it was not the pleasure but the anger that made her quiver.

Outside, a heavily polluted river rose and rolled southeast, turbulently. A spidery chain bridge stretched across it. Many times she heard that people had jumped from it; many nights she dreamed of that bridge, of leading her husband to its edge; she nudged him and he fell. Waking, she wouldn't call it a nightmare. Nothing could frighten a lonely woman unless it were the loneliness itself.

If doubts about her husband came across her mind at midnight, she did not allow herself to dwell on them for long. Spring was coming, she could get up to change the quilts, wash the winter jackets, or throw herself into every possible activity that needed a concentrated mind. This evening routine unchanged for the past seven years. For a lonely woman like her, daylight always came too late. Sometimes in the morning she found herself watching children play and chase one another, feeling happy that a red-cheeked boy bumped into her arms, asking for candy. And then it pained her as she realized she didn't have her own child.

On weekends, she had time to do whatever she wanted, having no parents to take care of. Her father died of heart disease when she was a teenager, and her mother, throwing away her life's labor, died two years later. In her memory, her mother was always in the kitchen, preparing food. Her father had lost his taste on account of medical malpractice. Everything her mother cooked, he would say, was too bland, and he would ask if there was anything else. Ma Dan was never allowed to eat her father's food. "Piggish girl, you should learn to cook for your man someday, or else there's the Buddhist nunnery waiting for girls who can't cook," her mother said, as if that explained everything.

It was the education she inherited from her mother that she needed to manage her own family one day, though now, except for housework, nothing needed her management, and the family, which consisted of herself most of the time, was no family at all. In Ma Dan's upbringing she had so many notions about marriage set in concrete. She was a wife, a daughter-in-law, a cleaner, a shopper, a cook, an ornament to the home, and a woman of ten thousand uses.

But it wasn't that once you married, you became someone's woman; you were no one's woman, then a lesser woman, and eventually, you felt you were no woman. Ma Dan no longer wore nice high heels and fancy bras to appeal to her husband or any men. What had she become? She even lost the courage to think of it.

Last Tuesday night, she took a different route home. It was lovely to make a bit of change and spend some time outside. Down the street, she paused at a fruit stand, saw an elderly woman asleep on her stall, and a vagrant pilfered four pears and fled. She had wanted to call out to someone to catch the thief, to wake the elderly woman, and to tell her what she had witnessed. As soon as Ma Dan's hand approached the owner's shoulder, she knew she couldn't do that. She quickly placed twenty yuan on the stand and walked down the narrow road.

A flickering slogan, RIDE ME UP TO HEAVEN, lured her into a sex toy shop. On the ceiling a globe of painted glass glistened and spun, throwing beams of light. There was music playing in the background. She stood quietly at the doorway, looking at the various sex organs displayed on the wall-mounted racks; her mind was racing, her throat craving water. Above all, a voice inside her told her to leave, but her feet seemed, of their own accord, to take her inside the shop.

"Anything you're interested in, let me know," said a man, coming out of the back room. He had a buzz cut and bloodshot eyes, and a tiger tattoo on his left shoulder. It might be due to the purple light that his skin looked cold, white, and sexy.

Standing there, she couldn't think of anything to say.

"There's nothing to feel embarrassed about," the man said. "Women sometimes do come to my shop, and some become return customers."

"What do you sell to ride men up to heaven?" She asked the

question before she knew she was asking it, and the fever rumbling in her head drowned her immediately.

The man, laughingly, turned out to be eloquent about his shop and the products, about his customers from prepubescent boys to grandfathers, about men and women, cars and houses, and his philosophy. The music relaxed Ma Dan and provoked her now and then into behavior that resembled nothing of herself.

"My whole life feels like an impotent penis," he said.

"You're very funny," she said.

"And you're laughing."

"I'm just smiling."

"Woman like you should laugh out loud."

Most of the time the man was doing the talking, cracking jokes, and she was listening and smiling, and her eyes, which before had been dull, sported a ripple of spark when she choked back giggling. When she was about to leave, the man wrapped up the dildo she had randomly chosen and gave her a special discount.

She thought she must be crazy.

When she came home, her husband was curled up on the sofa, checking his cell phone. He stayed there all night until he was called to sleep. There was very little talk in the bed, but that little consisted of the information that he would be on a five-day business trip, and she, in an attempt at intimacy, pressed her face on his shoulder, but he fell asleep very fast.

The next morning when her husband was in the bathroom, she noticed a brand-new pair of swim trunks and an unopened bottle of suntan oil in the open suitcase.

"What are you bringing the swim trunks for? Isn't it still cold in Beijing?"

"In case the hotel has a swimming pool."

"And in case the hotel has a sun so that you can use your sun-tan oil."

"Did you eat gunpowder for breakfast?"

All she had the following days was, again, herself and this empty room. She was annoyed with herself for always trying to find the good aspects of her marriage. Why would she expect him to change? She had married a man who had no feelings for women at all. There was no love. For the first time she thought about leaving him; she thought about money, her age, her educational background, and the elderly woman at the fruit stand. The idea died. Having been trapped in marriage for this long, she realized she could go nowhere and to nothing.

In the household as in any other place, men had the upper hand. Her mother, a country woman, had spent her life serving her father day and night so that when her father woke up at 3:00 a.m., demanding chicken soup, dumplings, and hot tea, her mother would jump on her feet and run to the kitchen. The clanking and clattering and the scent of fire would wake Ma Dan up; she would force her eyes not to open, not to listen to her father's displeasure with the food.

Every time Ma Dan felt the need to get up and defend her mother, she dared not. Her mother had told her not to. When the noise faded, they went into the bedroom, and she knew they had sex, though they'd made no sound. It was only a few minutes. She would stay awake, listening to her mother in the bathroom, washing; sometimes there was cigarette smoke, sometimes there was sobbing. One morning her mother killed a crucian carp, slapping its head with the back of the knife even after it stopped wriggling, as if easy death were too good for the fish. She turned around, startled, to see her daughter.

"Did I say you could scare me like this?"

"The chicken soup is too salty to eat."

"Didn't I tell you you should not eat your father's food?"

"You didn't make any breakfast this morning."

"You'll never eat your father's food again. Do you hear?"

"Yes."

Then her mother went outside to the yard, leaving the fish in the sink. She strode back in a moment later, a boiled egg in her bloodstained hand.

"Tell no one about the soup. Do you hear?"

"Yes."

IT WAS FRIDAY night once more. Lin Guofeng took a night off but didn't tell his wife. Sitting by the road and staring absently at the traffic for a long time, he forgot why he was there. At dusk, streetlamps lit up all of a sudden; old men were setting up tables under trees to play mahjong. He could hear their murmurs, complaining about their wives, but his concern was always of a different sort.

For a moment, Guofeng thought again of begging his boyfriend, who had discovered his marriage, to come back, and then, exhausted, he wanted nothing. Just hours earlier his boyfriend had moved out of the apartment Guofeng had rented for him. Guofeng was at work at the time and received the message—the key was on the hook behind the mailbox. Three months ago, on their trip to Hainan Island, his boyfriend decided that if he did not leave his wife, he would leave. That trip was supposed to be a celebration of their anniversary, and it was Guofeng's first time seeing the sea. There, they had walked along the beach, pressing their toes into the soft sand as waves bubbled around their ankles; and they went into the sea, letting the immense waves rock their bodies. The view was beautiful, but the tension was all wrong.

The moon, bright and fresh, had crossed the sleepy river and now mounted the highest building in the southeast. Putting his hands in his pants pockets, Guofeng immediately felt the key his boyfriend had returned to him. He took it out and flung it into the river.

He thought about his wife. To marry a woman was a decision he made; it was not due to his parents' power or relatives' opinions. He was then thirty-four and saw no point in living a gay life. On the other hand, he began to wonder, even consider, whether a woman could bring him the stable life he wanted. He distrusted boys but couldn't help falling for them.

So the woman, who had no parents and who had little experience with men, became the ideal choice, and with the stable life she provided, Guofeng could pursue his secret hunting.

MA DAN, LIPSTICKING her mouth in front of the mirror, was about to go to the sex toy shop. Friday nights had become an expectant part of her life. She texted the man earlier and asked if he had time to chat. He told her he had the entire night.

"I thought you wouldn't come today," the man said. Cigarette smoke hung in the air.

"Why wouldn't I?"

"It's already midnight."

"Better for me to do something at night than to wait for the sunrise," she said, realizing her mother had said this.

"That's where we've got something in common."

Then she described to him a friend of hers. She referred to the woman as her friend and tried to be as unemotional as she could in the telling, and all the time, the man was smiling.

"Do you think my friend is stupid?"

"I thought you were beautiful when you were talking about her."

And because he had said she was beautiful, she wanted him to keep that impression tonight. In fact, she had lost the habit of dressing up, almost forgot she was still in her thirties. Of her dresses, all that was not suitable for a housewife's look remained in the drawer, wrinkled and faded, and when she put on a floral dress that she had been unwilling to sell to secondhand stores, it made her smell like the drawer that hadn't been opened for a hundred years.

The man flicked the stub of his cigarette. "Let's walk."

He shut the rolling door and led the way down to the empty street. Always, he asked if she was tired and if they could go to his place. She said she would prefer to walk. He said he'd always wanted to walk like this because he was lonely most of the time, "just like your friend," he added.

If she hadn't lied, if lying wasn't always her first option, she would have told him she was the woman and that she was doing terrible. But she wasn't in the mood for another story tonight. They walked toward the direction of the river, through an underground passage, and emerged in an abandoned construction site.

"Come on," the man said, gripping her hand. "Be adventurous," he whispered in a tone of encouragement, and before she said yes, he led her in.

They walked through the tall grass, passed a dead pond, and came to a halt in front of the unfinished building. She could hear, not see, stray cats by some disturbance in the bush. This might be the place where they sheltered at night, mated when they were in heat, and died of natural causes at the end.

"Let's get out of here; I'm thirsty," she said.

At that, he hugged her, his tongue moisturizing her lips and parting them, invading new territory. His hand slid up the back of her dress and found its way between her legs. His fingers, like dry wood, were dampening her pubic hair. She sniffed the cigarette odor from his neck, deeply into her chest, drank it into her stomach. She felt the galloping of blood in his neck.

She surprised herself by making an orgasmic groan; she never thought such a sound could be made by her throat. She used to fake that sound to please her husband, though he never really enjoyed it.

The door of her body had been unconditionally opened. Now she only wanted that finger to crash her body, to battle, to wrestle.

Afterward, the man walked her home. At the front gate of the apartment complex, they hugged. The man gave her a long, wet kiss.

The wind howled in the darkness and threw petals onto their skins.

How strange and soft his tongue was.

She could see the bedroom window from where she stood, and it scared her, as if someone was watching in the dark. She buried her face in the man's chest. They had taken their time; he stroked her head and made her promise she would never do this with other men.

"We can meet every Friday night." She was not sure whether she really meant it, but it seemed the atmosphere demanded her to say that.

"I want to meet you every day!"

"I only have Friday nights."

"Oh, that's sad. I have every day and night."

When she went inside, she saw the lamplight glow from the bedroom and wondered if she had forgotten to turn it off. Tentatively, she pushed the door; her husband was smoking on the unmade bed. He raised his eyes, with something at once hard and yet a little impatient in the glance, and then no more.

When she was about to speak, he got up, put out the smoke, and asked if there was something to eat. She said she could cook, then went to the kitchen and heard her husband coughing. It sounded like he wasn't really coughing.

While he ate the noodles with gravy, the wife went to the bedroom. She had cooked this before, but he couldn't remember when. Ma Dan changed into pajamas, loosened her hair, and came out to sit beside her husband.

"You wear makeup in the middle of the night." Such a strange thing to say, such a strange laughter he let out.

She sat in silence, staring out the window, unable to see anything outside except a woman, a man, and a sulfur lamp projected on the window. If only he had asked her straight out, she wouldn't deny anything. With such performative silence between them, the stone in her heart grew heavier.

Guofeng had never thought that his wife was attractive to other men, that such a country woman would use his money to buy makeup. To keep his mouth busy, to give himself a moment of peace, he reached out for another cigarette and fiddled with a matchbox and then pulled an ashtray, making all rattle and jar. The ashes fell onto the ground. He tried to make things difficult for her, demanding a cup of hot tea and asking her to take out the trash right away.

He didn't know what to do with his feelings and didn't understand what the feelings were. Tomorrow he might spend some time in another apartment, call the landlord, and cancel the lease, or he might leave it until the end of this month. After all, everyone needed time to think.

Another day came as usual, hot and damp. Guofeng got up very early. When he went out, the wife turned on the air conditioner and slept until the afternoon. In bed, she thought about the man and his kiss. His words echoed in her head as she clutched the pillow tightly in her arms. She also remembered her mother telling her that any man who said *love* so easily wanted something else from her.

Guofeng spent more time at home, even on weekends when he didn't have to work. He praised her cooking, began going to the supermarket with her, and sometimes spent money on expensive Japanese sea fish and Chilean cherries. When autumn came, he bought Yangcheng Lake hairy crabs, despite his wife saying she had no idea how to handle them.

So much of his life had revolved around things that he would doubt, but never his marriage. Sometimes, lying in bed and listening to the breath of his wife, Guofeng wondered if he really had no feelings for women; he tried and failed, as he always did.

The other night when Guofeng was about to sleep, he discovered a dildo, which was wrapped in a plastic bag and placed in the bottom of the drawer. He looked at it with doubt; he didn't remember buying it himself, but on second thought, he knew it belonged to his wife. It was a mockery, a slap in his face. When he went in search of Ma Dan, he found the door to the bathroom locked and no sound was in it, and a half hour later when he called out her name, heard only the water flushing in reply.

ONE NIGHT WHEN Guofeng was crossing the chain bridge, he saw all the lights in his apartment were turned on. At the door, he recognized his parents' shoes; there was a draft coming from inside—judging from the smell, it must be chicken soup. On the table, a hot pot cooker was spewing steam into the ceiling. Guofeng, wondering why they were here so late, took his shoes off and went to the kitchen.

"Don't touch anything," his mother said, rinsing millet in a bowl. His father lifted the lid of the pot, put the pitted date and sliced Chinese yam into the soup all at once, smiled to Guofeng, revealing his tawny teeth.

He ladled up some soup and asked his son to taste it.

Guofeng blew the broth, sipped it, and smacked his lips. "Did you forget to put salt?"

"Salt isn't good for her; there's no need," his mother said.

"It isn't your birthday today, is it, Mother?"

The old woman laughed out loud. "Your wife is pregnant." When the dinner was ready, his mother woke Ma Dan up.

"I feel nauseated and have no appetite to eat," she said, her voice husky as if she'd sobbed.

"It's for the baby; now you eat for two people." The mother giggled.

During the dinner Guofeng's father talked about names, saying he would consult a reputable fortune teller.

"According to our genealogy, the baby should have the character Zheng in his given name. How about Lin Zhengyi?"

"Who still believes that?" Guofeng said as he turned to face his wife.

Ma Dan only stared at her bowl, not saying anything.

"I'm so happy to have my grandchild before I go to heaven. Dan, you're the big hero of our family," Guofeng's mother said.

"My mother didn't have the luck to see my baby," Ma Dan said. Now she really missed her mother and could think of no one else but her mother to tell her what to do. The mention made her nose twitch.

"Your mother should be so proud of you," Guofeng's mother said, picking up a piece of pork and placing it into her bowl. "I kept thinking about my youth. I was twenty-two and working in the cotton mill. Then the child was born, then your father joined the army, then the State-owned enterprises were restructured, layoffs began, and I lost my job. My parents were old, and there were three hungry mouths to feed at home. I was on my own; no one could help. I wasn't sure why this baby arrived so late, I thought perhaps you weren't ready, but every time I came and saw how you kept this old apartment clean and neat, and I saw the food in the kitchen and things, I knew you're a good wife and you'll be a responsible mother."

Ma Dan was quiet. She held back her story, feeling the mother's kindness in her eyes. You couldn't blame a good mother for everything, she thought.

Guofeng, without a word, buried his head into the bowl, eating.

His parents kept on the subject of names for a while, then the subject of the hospital, and then of school. There was some bickering here and there, but in the bickering was laughter, was satisfaction, was pride.

Guofeng spent every day at work. Some nights when he got back, his wife was not home. He called, but her cell phone rang on the sofa. He took a hot shower and watched TV until it was late and he realized he needed to find her. He stepped out onto the street and discovered it had snowed.

The wind had rubbed away all signs of autumn; frost had carpeted the ground. No one would come out on such a cold night. Ma Dan felt tired. She felt that she hadn't slept for a very long time, and now her body was light as if the baby was leaving her. She put her hand on her belly and felt nothing. She came to the very edge of the river, unbuttoned her coat, closed her eyes, and remembered the tall grass, the summer heat, and how cool his breath felt on her skin. Let me get sick, she thought, and she cursed her baby.

She had told the man about the baby and waited for his love. He said business was slow and that his shop had come to an end. He told her he was leaving for Guangzhou, where there were more opportunities.

"When I get settled and make some money and everything, I'll take you and the baby to live with me," he said.

She pressed no further, knowing, with an unexpected sense of shame, not to jeopardize her hope.

In the moonlight, they walked along the river, the man's eyes gleaming in a way that she once recognized in her husband. They hugged, his back to the river, and she felt a cold breath on her neck. When she led his hand to touch her belly, he seemed not to want to touch it. He didn't stroke her head or kiss her as he used to. In certain light, she saw herself in the man's eyes; in certain light, she looked so much like her mother. She knew that their relationship was a nocturnal thing that never survived daylight. Behind them, the river was rapidly freezing. And an absurd voice in her mind told her to push the man into the river. "Push him! It's easy," she thought. "Just push him! Go after him, you and your baby." She listened to the crack of the ice, unsettling.

She had this recurring dream during the day while dozing off on the sofa. Waking up, she heard children skating on the ice, and her back was all wet. Since being pregnant, she began to look ill, kept the chopsticks suspended when eating, and came down with frequent fevers. The only sound Guofeng heard her make the whole day was when she counted the fetal movements and she would groan *Lambkin*.

Guofeng was smoking on the balcony; cold air drifted back into the living room, where there were baby posters on the walls. He stood there watching mothers or grandmothers absorbed in their kids, who were throwing snowballs at each other, and imagining the lives of three people in this apartment. He was a little nervous; small creatures made him afraid. He never failed to kick a toy or a snowball out of his way fiercely, had waited until his wife stopped going out at night before he felt secure enough to begin loving the baby. He liked the name his father suggested from the genealogy, though it sounded unfashionable.

At the bottom of his heart, he could not help worrying that one day the baby would find out he was not his father. He wouldn't explain anything, but he would give him as much of the world as he had. Just that. He would hold in private how it felt when a father did not want his child to be born into this world.

He wondered what story the mother would tell the child. He wouldn't want her to tell the truth, because truth had the power of ravaging. But that was not the matter at hand. The coldest day of January was coming, making the night shift more difficult. Whenever the baby was born, his superior at the Railway Bureau agreed to transfer him to another post so that he could spend every Friday night at home.

He lingered on the balcony for a while and considered enclosing it with casement windows and buying some foam pads for the floor. When he went in, he saw his wife lying on the couch, eyes to the ceiling, tears on her face. She quickly wiped them away as she saw him. He went to the kitchen and poured her a cup of warm water, holding it with both hands as if there was no turbulence in his heart.

She drank the water in one gulp. Rubbing his hands warmly, Guofeng put her right leg on his knee, took off her long socks, and began to rub her swollen calf. She flinched at first, but he insisted. It was the first time he touched her feet. He noticed the faded toenail polish, knowing she had done so to please the man.

A small life was living in her body; he didn't feel it real until he touched her rapidly growing belly and the baby gave back movements.

The boundaries of skin seemed gone.

He kept on massaging the knots that appeared on her instep, his thumb pushing deep toward the collateral channels. The tension in her legs began to loosen, as if something locked inside was oozing out.

Without any warning, tears started to roll down her cheeks.

"Does that hurt?" he asked.

She shook her head, swallowing the sob.

"You can let it out; there's no need to hold back."

She had her head buried in the cushions, her Venus dimples now exposed when she curled herself up.

He got up, drew down all the curtains, and snapped off the light. The day shifted to night.

"Does that feel any better?"

Guofeng didn't know that one can cry so much and can contain so much. He caught up her hand in his and she inhaled deeply. When her breathing became easier, she decided to tell her story. She started with the night in the sex toy shop, and then the dildo, telling him how it slid into her body, giving her a taste of happiness, and how it gently, slyly crashed her life.

Zhenglong Yang was born and raised in China, trained at university to be "the tongue and throat" of the Communist Party. He came to America after twelve years of serving as a host in a state-owned TV station. He has taught creative writing at University of Texas at Austin, where he is an MFA candidate with the New Writers Project.

About the Judges

LYDI CONKLIN is the author of the novel *Songs of No Provenance* and the story collection *Rainbow Rainbow*, which was long-listed for the Story Prize and the PEN/Robert W. Bingham Prize for Debut Short Story Collection. Their fiction has appeared in *Tin House*, *American Short Fiction*, and *The Paris Review*. They've drawn comics for *The New Yorker*, *The Believer*, *Lenny Letter*, and other publications.

DIONNE IRVING is a writer from Toronto, Ontario. She is the author of the novel *Quint* and the story collection *The Islands*. Her work has appeared in *Story*, *Boulevard*, *Literary Hub*, *Missouri Review*, and *New Delta Review*, among other journals and magazines. Irving teaches in the creative writing program and the Initiative on Race and Resilience at the University of Notre Dame.

BRENDA PEYNADO is the author of the story collection *The Rock Eaters*. Peynado has won an O. Henry Award, a Pushcart Prize, the *Chicago Tribune*'s Nelson Algren Literary Award, selection for *The Best American Science Fiction and Fantasy* and *The Best Small Fictions*, a Dana Award, a Fulbright grant to the Dominican Republic, and other awards. Her fiction appears in *The Georgia Review*, *The Sun* magazine, *The Southern Review*, *The Kenyon Review*, *The Threepenny Review*, *Prairie Schooner*, and more than forty other journals.

About the PEN/Robert J. Dau Short Story Prize for Emerging Writers

The PEN/Robert J. Dau Short Story Prize for Emerging Writers recognizes twelve fiction writers for a debut short story published in a print or online literary magazine. The annual award was offered for the first time during PEN America's 2017 literary awards cycle. The twelve winning stories are selected by a committee of three judges. The writers of the stories each receive a $2,000 cash prize and are honored at the annual PEN America Literary Awards Ceremony in New York City. Every year, Catapult publishes the winning stories in *Best Debut Short Stories: The PEN America Dau Prize*. This award is generously supported by the family of the late Robert J. Dau, whose commitment to the literary arts has made him a fitting namesake for this career-launching prize. Mr. Dau was born and raised in Petoskey, a city in Northern Michigan close in proximity to Walloon Lake, where Ernest Hemingway spent his summers as a young boy and which serves as the backdrop for Hemingway's *The Torrents of Spring*. Petoskey is also known as the site where Hemingway determined that he would commit to becoming a writer. This proximity to literary history ignited the Dau family's interest in promoting emerging voices in fiction and spotlighting the next great fiction writers.

List of Participating Publications

After Dinner Conversation
AGNI
The Arkansas International
The Common
Conjunctions
The Dodge
Efiko Magazine
FIYAH Magazine of Black Speculative Fiction
The Florida Review
Foglifter
The Georgia Review
HAD
Hearth & Coffin Literary Journal
HEAT
The Hopkins Review
Kinsman Quarterly
L'Esprit Literary Review
McSweeney's Quarterly
Michigan Quarterly Review
Midwest Review
The Montréal Review
n+1
North American Review
Notch Magazine
Oyster River Pages

Peatsmoke Journal

Ploughshares

Porter House Review

Radon Journal

Split Lip Magazine

StoryQuarterly

Tint Journal

Vocivia Magazine

Wallstrait

Permissions

PEN America stands at the intersection of literature and human rights to protect open expression in the United States and worldwide. The organization champions the freedom to write, recognizing the power of the word to transform the world. Its mission is to unite writers and their allies to celebrate creative expression and defend the liberties that make it possible. Learn more at pen.org.

01 14